BiG NATE

BACK TO BACK HITS

D1176176

ALSO BY LINCOLN PEIRCE

Big Nate: In a Class by Himself
Big Nate Strikes Again
Big Nate Flips Out
Big Nate: In the Zone
Big Nate Lives It Up
Big Nate Blasts Off

Big Nate: What Could Possibly Go Wrong?
Big Nate: Here Goes Nothing
Big Nate: Genius Mode
Big Nate: Mr. Popularity

Big Nate Boredom Buster
Big Nate Fun Blaster
Big Nate Doodlepalooza
Big Nate Laugh-O-Rama
Big Nate Super Scribbler
Big Nate Puzzlemania

Big Nate: Double Trouble

Lincoln Peirce

BiG NATE
BACK TO BACK HITS

BALZER + BRAY
An Imprint of HarperCollins*Publishers*

ISBN 978-0-06-294209-8

Typography by Sasha Illingworth
19 20 21 22 23   PC/LSCH   10 9 8 7 6 5 4 3 2 1
❖
First Edition

BIG NATE

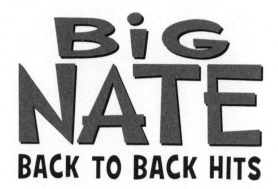

BACK TO BACK HITS

Lincoln Peirce

BiG NATE

ON A ROLL

For Dana H.P., my good one.

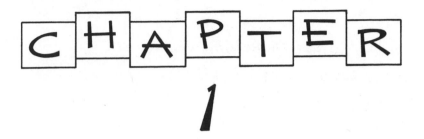

CHAPTER 1

I never really noticed before how boring the detention room is.

I guess that's not exactly breaking news. Any room where the main activities are (1) sitting quietly with your head on the desk or (2) writing "I will not make vulgar noises dur-  ing Mary Ellen Popowski's flute performance" a hundred times isn't exactly Thrillsville.

(By the way, I'm not here because I made vulgar noises during Mary Ellen Popowski's flute perfor- mance. That was last week. And it wasn't even on purpose!)

What I mean is, the room ITSELF is boring. The only things on the wall are two signs. One says QUIET, PLEASE and the other—just in case anybody's too dense to figure out sign #1—says NO TALKING. I'm not expecting them to have a TV in here or anything, but would it kill them to put up a couple of posters?

See how it took her a second to answer? She's all wrapped up in one of her cheesy romance novels.

"Can I zip down to the art studio for a sec?"

She raises an eyebrow. "The art studio? What for?"

Down goes the eyebrow. "Nate," she says, "P.S. 38 has no interest in 'jazzing up' the detention room."

"Exactly!" I answer.

Okay, so much for that idea. Guess Mrs. C.'s in one of her no-nonsense moods. Sometimes she's a little more chatty, but that's usually when it's just her and me. Today there are three other kids in here:

NAME: *Seth Quincy*
WHY HE'S HERE: *He got so mad at a bunch of kids for calling him Q-tip, he totally snapped. Personally, I think it's kind of a cool nickname, but that's just me.*

NAME: *Lee Ann Pfister*
WHY SHE'S HERE: *She broke the rule that says you can't wear shirts or blouses that show off your belly button. Not only that, she has an outie.*

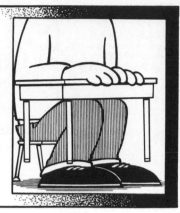

NAME: *Chester Budrick*
WHY HE'S HERE: *He wanted to trade lunches with Eric Fleury, but Eric said no. So Chester stuffed a hot dog up Eric's nose. Did I mention Chester is kind of a psycho?*

And then there's me. You probably want to know how I ended up here. Well, that makes two of us. It wasn't my fault. Not even CLOSE. It was pretty much all ARTUR'S doing. And of course I got detention while Artur, aka Mr. Lucky, got absolutely nothing! It's sort of a long story.

...BUT I GUESS I'VE GOT PLENTY OF TIME...

SKWEE! SKWEE! SKWEE!

... SO I'LL GO AHEAD AND **TELL** IT!

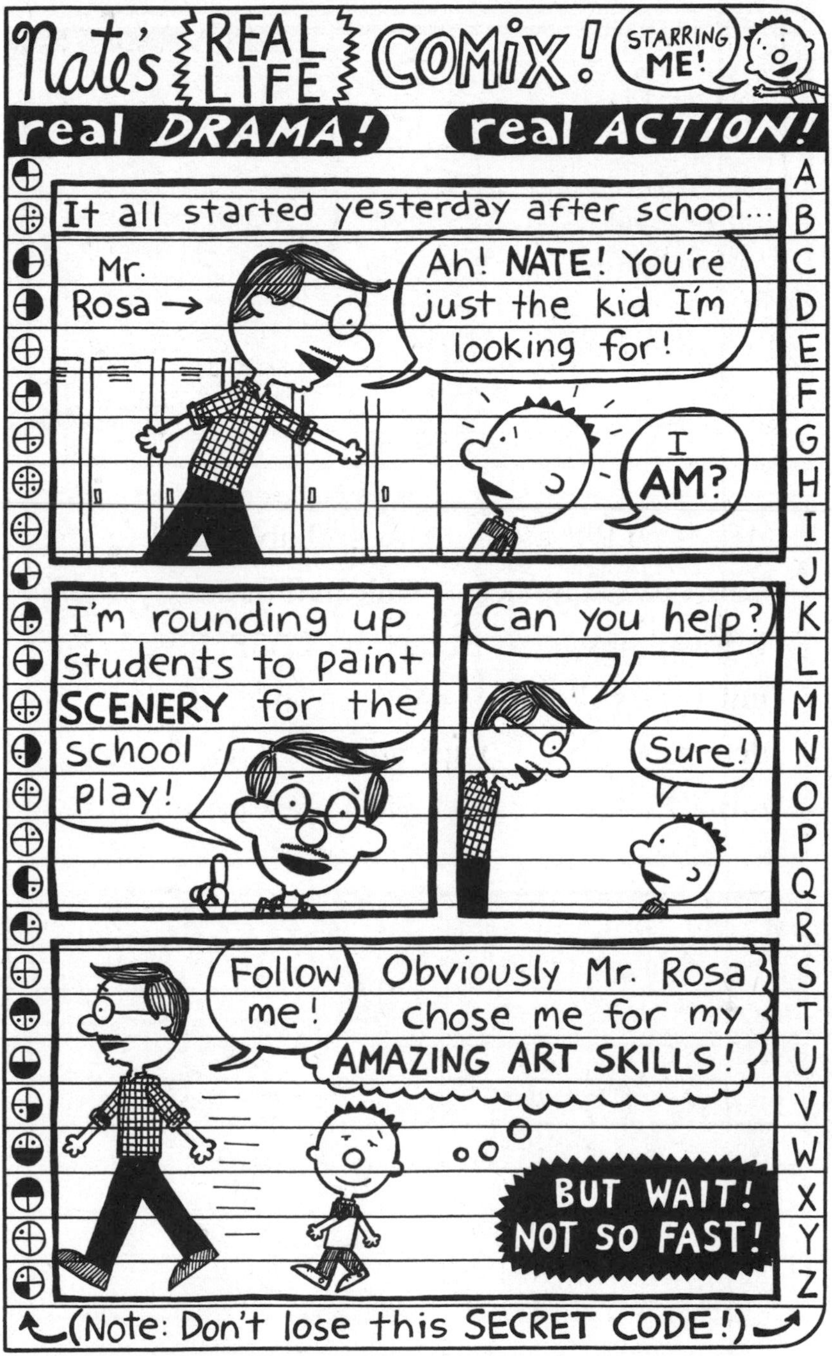
Nate's REAL LIFE COMIX!
STARRING ME!
real DRAMA! real ACTION!
It all started yesterday after school...
Mr. Rosa →
Ah! NATE! You're just the kid I'm looking for!
I AM?
I'm rounding up students to paint SCENERY for the school play!
Can you help?
Sure!
Follow me!
Obviously Mr. Rosa chose me for my AMAZING ART SKILLS!
BUT WAIT! NOT SO FAST!
A B C D E F G H I J K L M N O P Q R S T U V W X Y Z
(Note: Don't lose this SECRET CODE!)

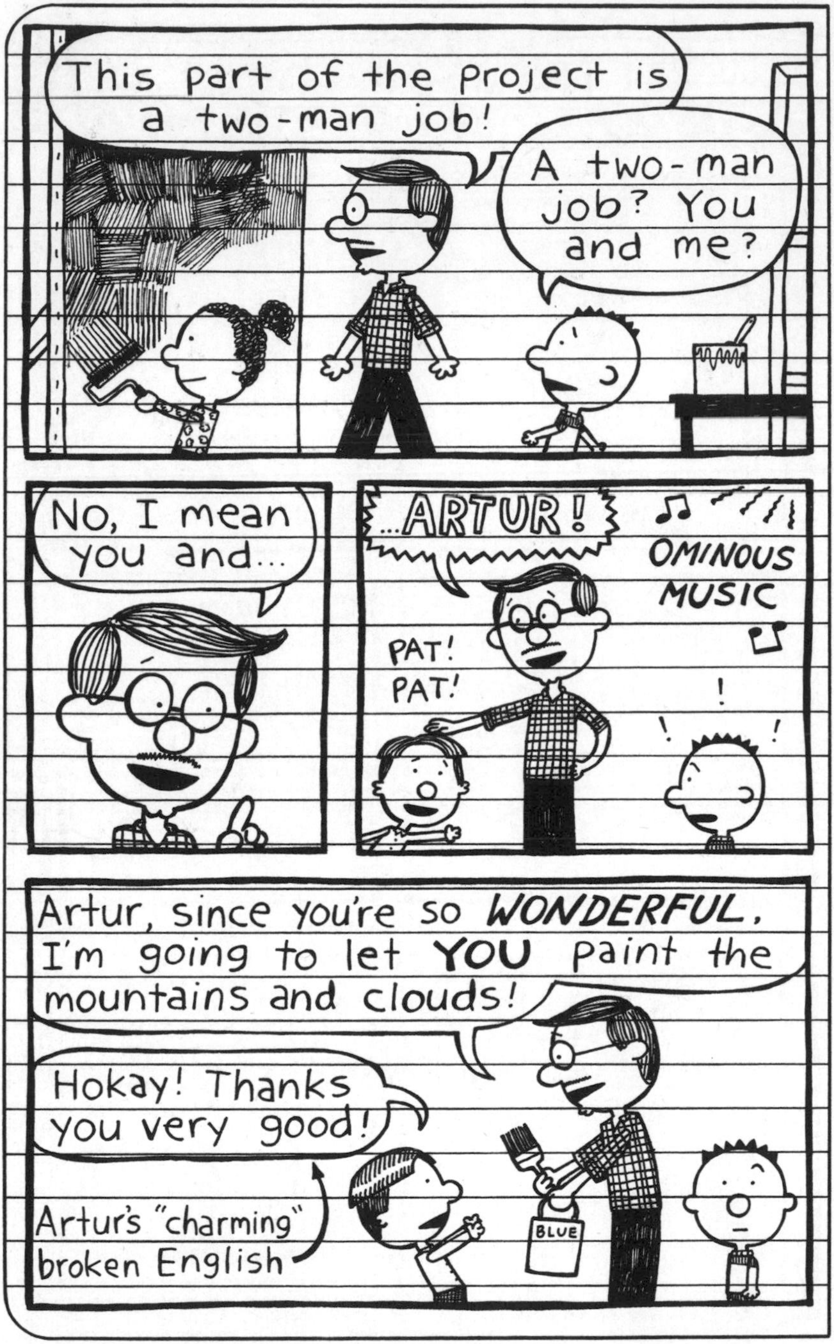
This part of the project is a two-man job!
A two-man job? You and me?
No, I mean you and...
...ARTUR!
OMINOUS MUSIC
PAT! PAT!
!
! !
Artur, since you're so WONDERFUL, I'm going to let YOU paint the mountains and clouds!
Hokay! Thanks you very good!
Artur's "charming" broken English
BLUE

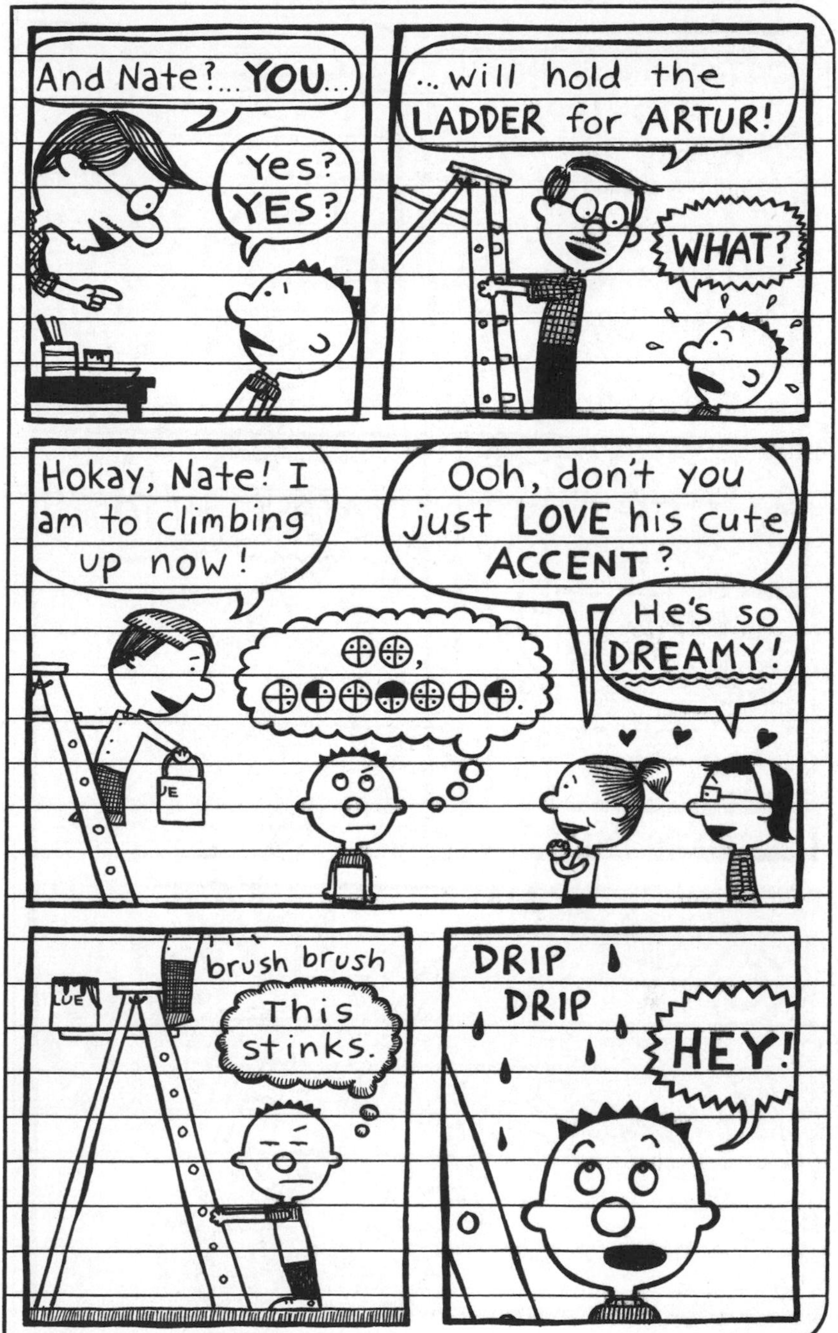
And Nate?... **YOU**...
Yes? YES?
...will hold the LADDER for ARTUR!
WHAT?
Hokay, Nate! I am to climbing up now!
Ooh, don't you just **LOVE** his cute **ACCENT**?
He's so DREAMY!
brush brush
This stinks.
DRIP
DRIP
HEY!

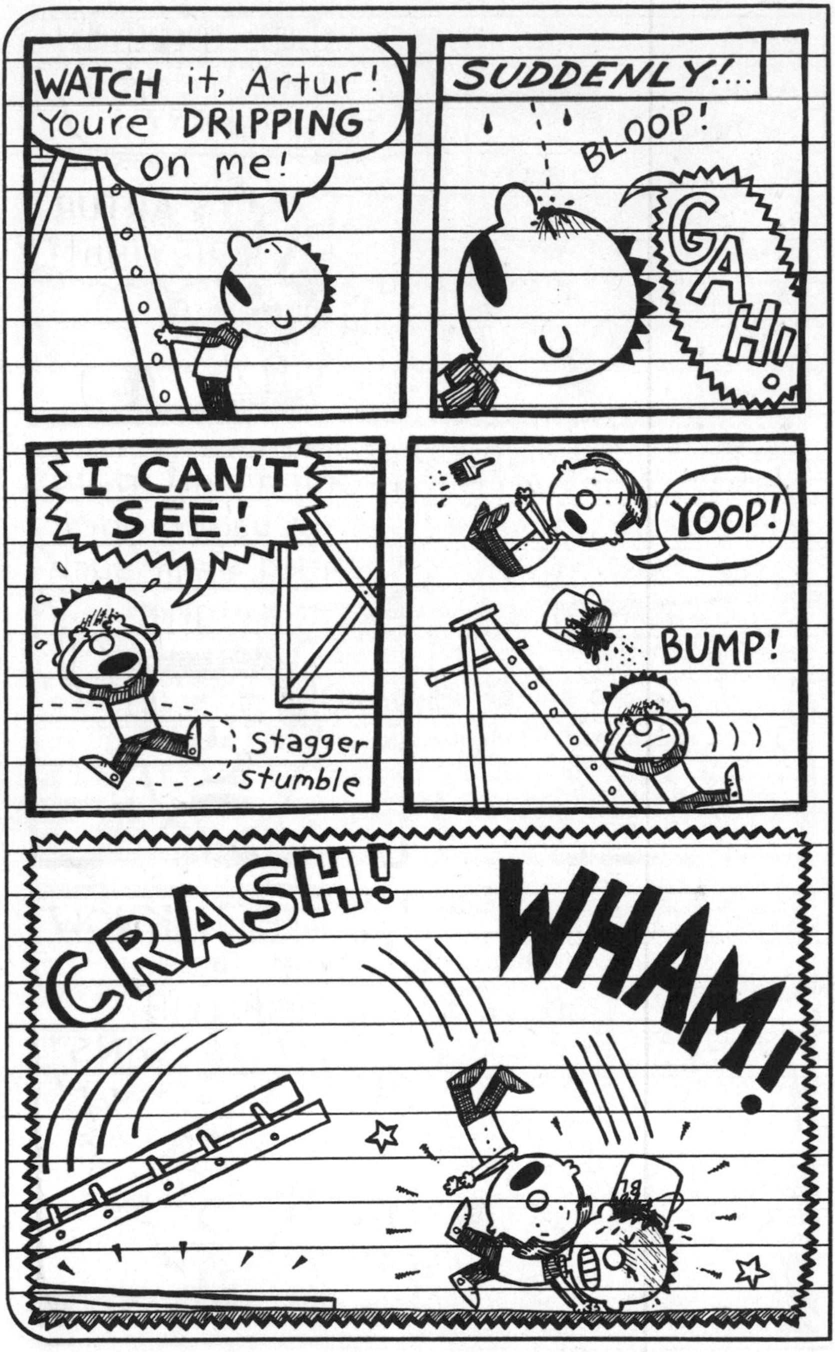
WATCH it, Artur! You're DRIPPING on me!
SUDDENLY!...
BLOOP!
GAH!
I CAN'T SEE!
stagger
stumble
YOOP!
BUMP!
CRASH!
WHAM!

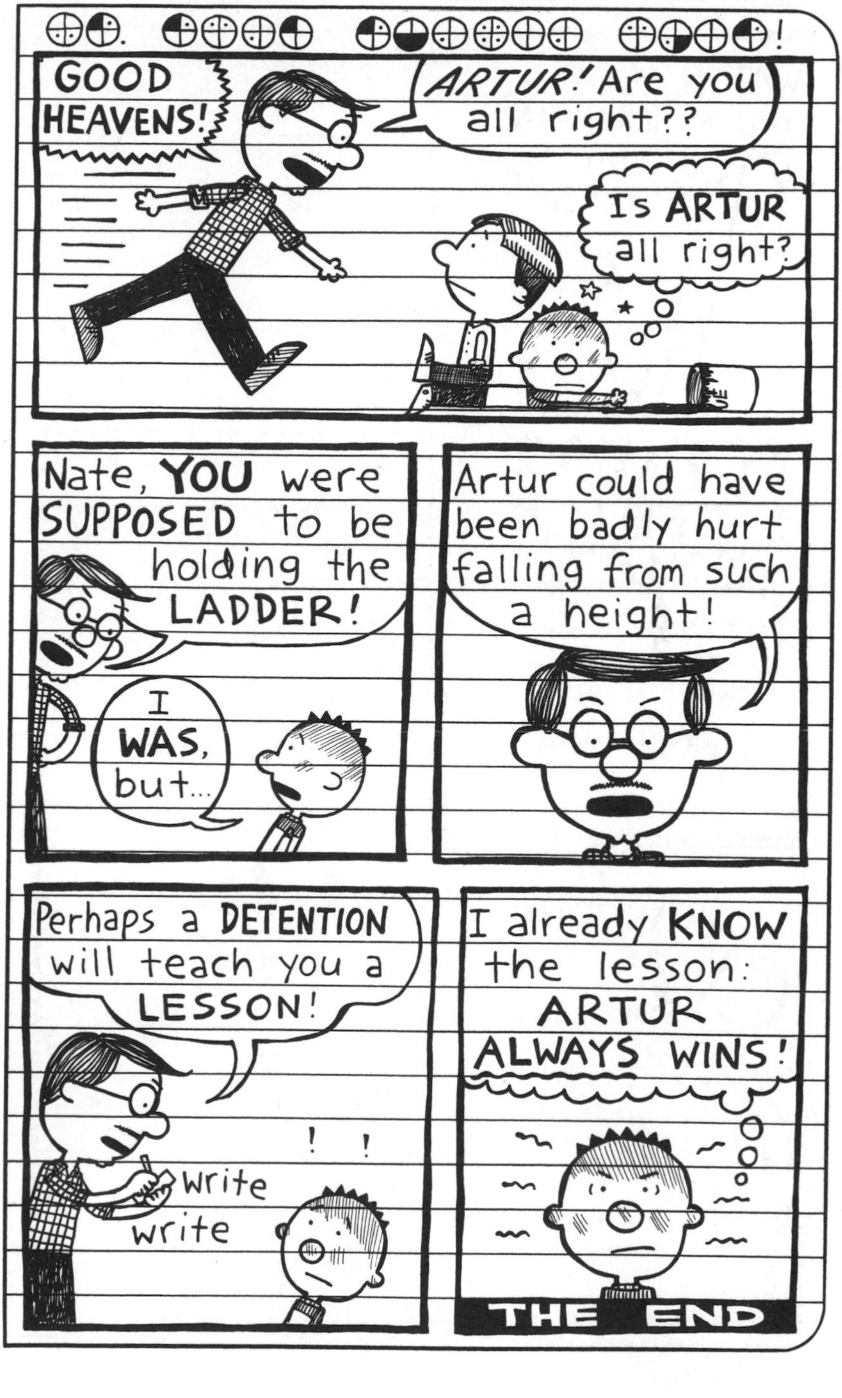
GOOD HEAVENS!
ARTUR! Are you all right??
Is ARTUR all right?
Nate, YOU were SUPPOSED to be holding the LADDER!
I WAS, but...
Artur could have been badly hurt falling from such a height!
Perhaps a DETENTION will teach you a LESSON!
write write
! !
I already KNOW the lesson: ARTUR ALWAYS WINS!
THE END

It's true: He DOES always win. Let's face it, Artur has everything going for him. He's friendly, he's smart, he's good at practically everything. All the teachers love him, and so do the kids. Hey, even I like him, and I can't stand the guy.

Want to know what else is annoying? Because I got detention—which, just so we're clear on this, was thanks to Artur—I'm going to be late for my Timber Scout meeting.

Yup. I'm a scout. I used to want nothing to do with scouting, because every time Francis and Teddy came back from a Timber Scout camping trip, they always had food poisoning. Or worse.

But they finally convinced me to give it a try. It's not as dorky as I thought it might be. There are a few lame parts, but those are balanced out by the good stuff. Like the uniform. The uniform rocks.

Even the beret is kind of cool. I have to admit, before I joined the Timber Scouts, I thought the only people who wore berets were French guys and mimes.

Anyway, the stinkin' meeting's already started. Maybe I can make the second half of it. MAYBE! . . .

YES! I explode out of my chair, race down the hallway to my locker, grab my uniform, and duck into the bathroom to change. Thirty seconds later, and . . .

Teddy's dad is our troop leader, so our meetings are always at his place. It's a fifteen-minute walk from here . . .

I strap on my helmet and push off. I zip along Haywood Avenue, turn left onto Pepper Street, and start across the bridge over Beard's Creek—which really isn't a creek. It's more like a combination swamp and garbage dump.

There's a woman walking her dog up ahead. Well, maybe "dog" isn't the right word. It's one of those toy poodles that looks like somebody glued cotton balls to a weasel. I mean, if you're going to have a dog like that, why not just get a CAT?

The woman moves to her left when she hears me coming. But the dog goes the other way. Before I can slow down, her leash is stretched across the sidewalk like a trip wire, and I'm heading straight into it.

WHAM!

I sort of flip while I'm falling, so I end up landing on my backpack. That's the good news. The bad news is, my skateboard keeps going. It shoots under the bridge railing, dive-bombs into the creek . . .

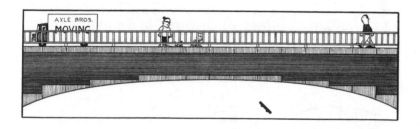

. . . and sinks into the oily water. Good-bye, skateboard.

SPLOOSH!

The dog's yapping, the woman's babbling, and people are rubbernecking as they drive by. But I can't focus on any of it. I think maybe I'm in shock. All I can do is look down at the ripples in the water where my board disappeared. Forever.

I take off my helmet in disgust and stuff it in my backpack. No more riding.

This whole disaster is one big Artur chain reaction. If he hadn't spilled paint on me, I wouldn't have (1) bumped into the ladder, (2) landed in detention, (3) been late to my

Timber Scout meeting, (4) ridden my skateboard to Teddy's house, (5) crashed into that lady and her dog, and (6) lost my board in the creek. See how it all fits together? Thanks a LOT, Artur.

It takes a while, but I finally get to Teddy's house. The guys are sitting on the front steps.

"Oh, really?" I mumble. Frankly, at this point I'm too exhausted to care.

"AND . . ." Francis says with a huge smile, "our troop has some great news!"

Great news? I perk up a little bit.

"We just initiated a new member!" Teddy announces.

Francis rattles off a fake drumroll. Teddy does his crowd noise sound effect. The door swings open, and . . .

THIS is supposed to be great news??

CHAPTER 2

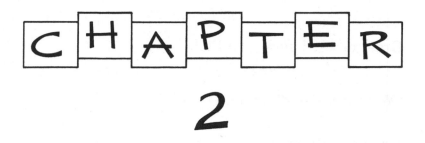

"How do I looks in my costume, guys?" he asks.

COSTUME?? It's a UNIFORM, you pinhead!

"You look awesome, Artur," says Francis.

Right. Of COURSE he looks awesome. Why WOULDN'T he? After all . . .

"How come you're making that weird face?" Teddy asks me.

"Maybe you are have gas," Artur suggests.

"I'm bummed out about missing the meeting, that's all."

Nobody says anything. Hey, fine by me. There's nothing they could say to make me feel much better, anyway.

Except THAT!

"Uh . . . hold it," says Teddy. "There actually aren't any left."

Oh, really? So Peachy McWonderful gets what should have been MINE? SHOCKER!

"Sorry," says Teddy sheepishly.

Hey, no biggie. I'll just starve to death, that's all. Besides, a cookie can't fix my REAL problem: I just blew my chance to get my attendance merit badge.

In Timber Scouts, there are merit badges for just about everything. Here are some of the ones I've earned so far:

☑ **HELPING HANDS** – You're supposed to do good deeds without getting paid anything. So I took care of Spitsy, the dog next door, while Mr. Eustis was at a polka festival in Buffalo.

Turns out Spitsy had an intestinal virus that week. No wonder Mr. Eustis left town.

☑ **FIRST AID** – The hardest part wasn't learning CPR, making splints, or tying a jillion tourniquets. It was practicing the Heimlich Maneuver on Chad.

☑ **ARTS & CRAFTS** – This was the easiest badge to earn, **BY FAR.** All you have to do is spend ten hours working on some sort of art project.

Hey, **I** spend that much time drawing "DOCTOR CESSPOOL" comics nearly *EVERY WEEK!*

↓   ↓   ↓

Don't miss the **NEXT ISSUE!**
STARRING...

Our HERO!	His trusty NURSE!	His bitter RIVAL!

Doctor Cesspool!	Maureen Biology!	Dr. Arch Enemy!

○ **BADGES I'M CLOSE TO EARNING:**
Attendance, Citizenship, Orienteering, Archery, Knot Tying, Conservation, Swimming, Public Speaking

○ **BADGES I DON'T WANT TO EARN:**
Nutrition (because I'd have to give up Cheez Doodles), Bugling, Taxidermy, Sewing, Tap Dancing

Anyway, let me get back to the whole attendance badge thing. To earn one, you have to go to every single weekly meeting for six months—or at least PART of every meeting. Teddy's dad always explains it like this:

Six months is twenty-six meetings in a row. Here's the killer: Today's meeting WOULD have been number twenty-five.

"Ah!" says Artur, pointing at a car pulling into Teddy's driveway. "There is my mom!"

He motions to me and Francis. "Jump into, guys! We will give to you rides home!"

"No, thanks. I'd rather walk," I say right away. Actually, a ride would be great. If ARTUR wasn't in the car.

Good ol' Francis.

We wave good-bye to Teddy and start home. Francis lives right next to me, so it's the same trip for both of us.

"Where's your skateboard?" he asks after a while. "Didn't you bring it to school today?"

So much for THAT line of questioning. I'm not trying to be a jerk or anything. I just don't feel like talking about it right now.

"Well then, how 'bout a little trivia?" Francis asks cheerfully. I groan, but it's too late. He's already pulled out that stupid book, and he's flipping through it with sort of a crazed look in his eyes.

"Ready?" he asks.

"Nope," I answer. Hey, I've got to be honest.

"Try another question," I say. "That one's too easy."

"Okay," he says, clearing his throat. "What astro-physicist was responsible for—?"

"I was KIDDING, Einstein," I tell him.

"Well, mostly we talked about our fund-raiser," he says.

"They're wall hangings with little sayings on them," he explains. "Take a look."

He hands me a brochure. I scan the page. Wait, is this a JOKE?

"They are pretty bad," Francis admits.

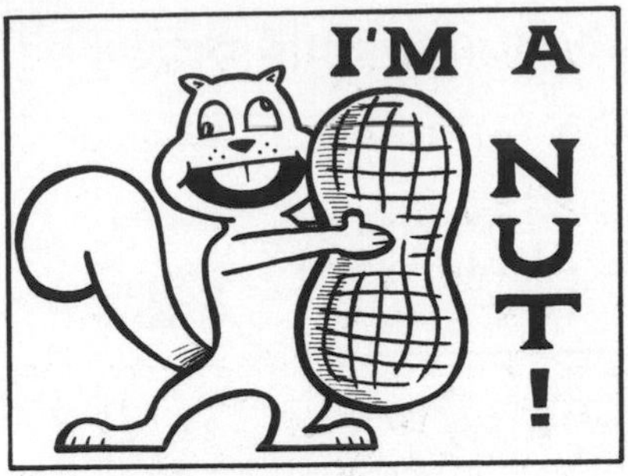
I'M A NUT!

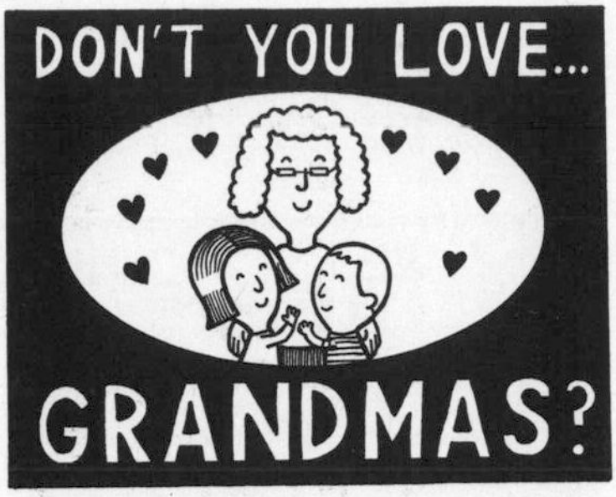
DON'T YOU LOVE...
GRANDMAS?

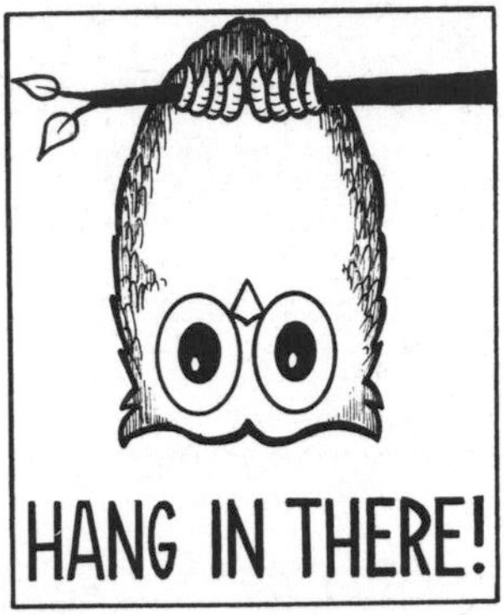
HANG IN THERE!

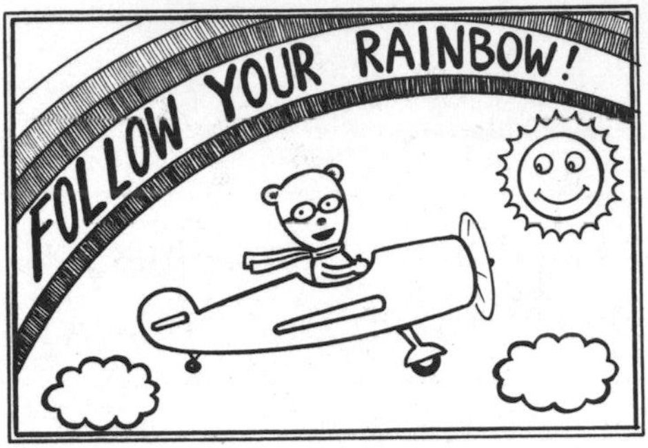
FOLLOW YOUR RAINBOW!

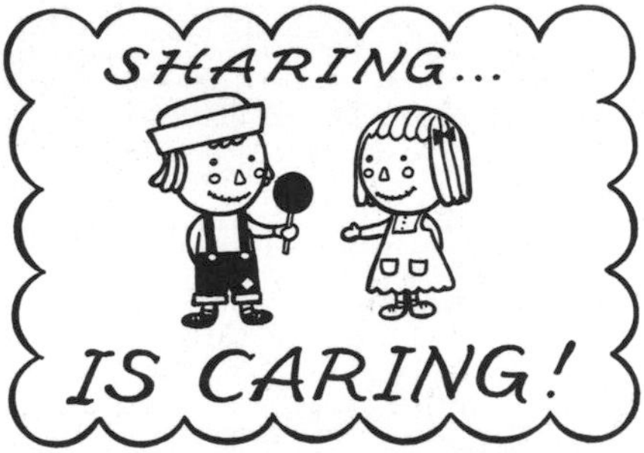
SHARING...
IS CARING!

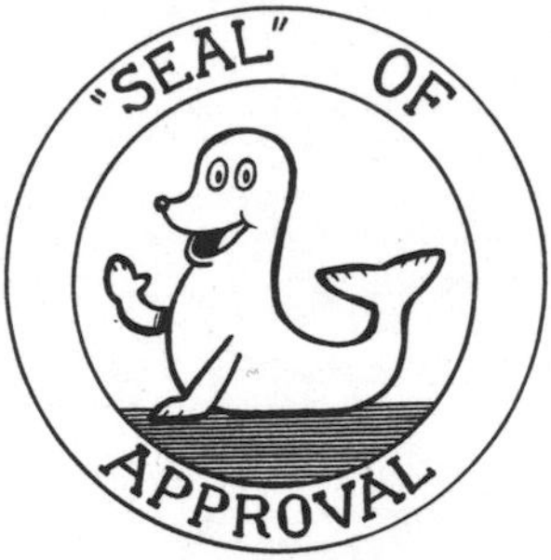
"SEAL" OF
APPROVAL

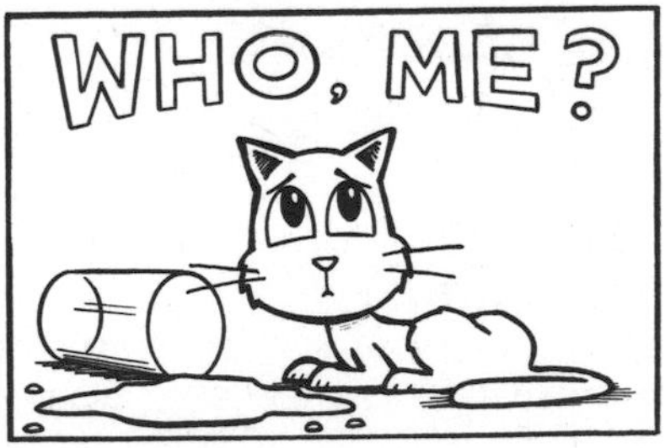
WHO, ME?

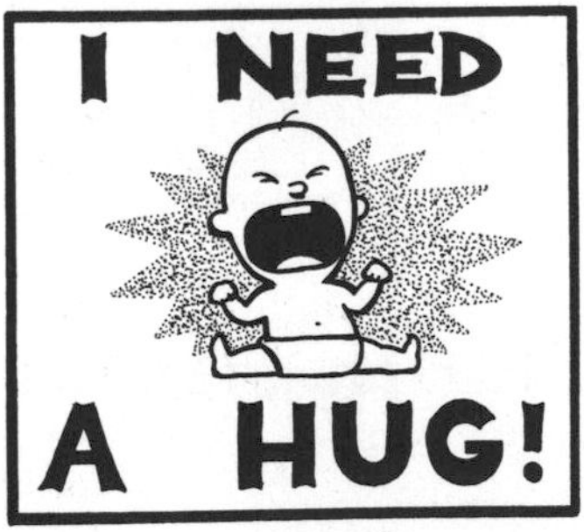
I NEED
A HUG!

I've sold stuff door-to-door before, but never anything THIS lame. This Warm Fuzzies thing is going to end up somewhere on my list of . . .

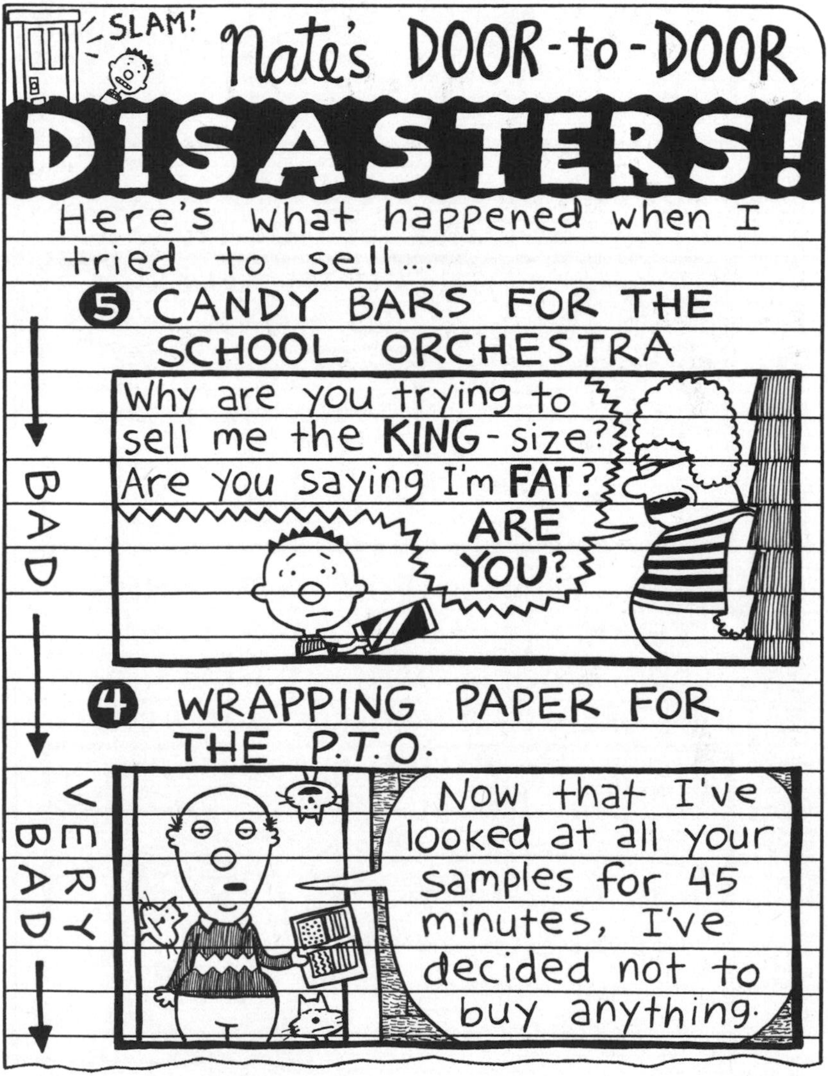
SLAM!
Nate's DOOR-to-DOOR
DISASTERS!
Here's what happened when I tried to sell...
5 CANDY BARS FOR THE SCHOOL ORCHESTRA
Why are you trying to sell me the KING-size? Are you saying I'm FAT?
ARE YOU?
BAD
4 WRAPPING PAPER FOR THE P.T.O.
Now that I've looked at all your samples for 45 minutes, I've decided not to buy anything.
VERY BAD

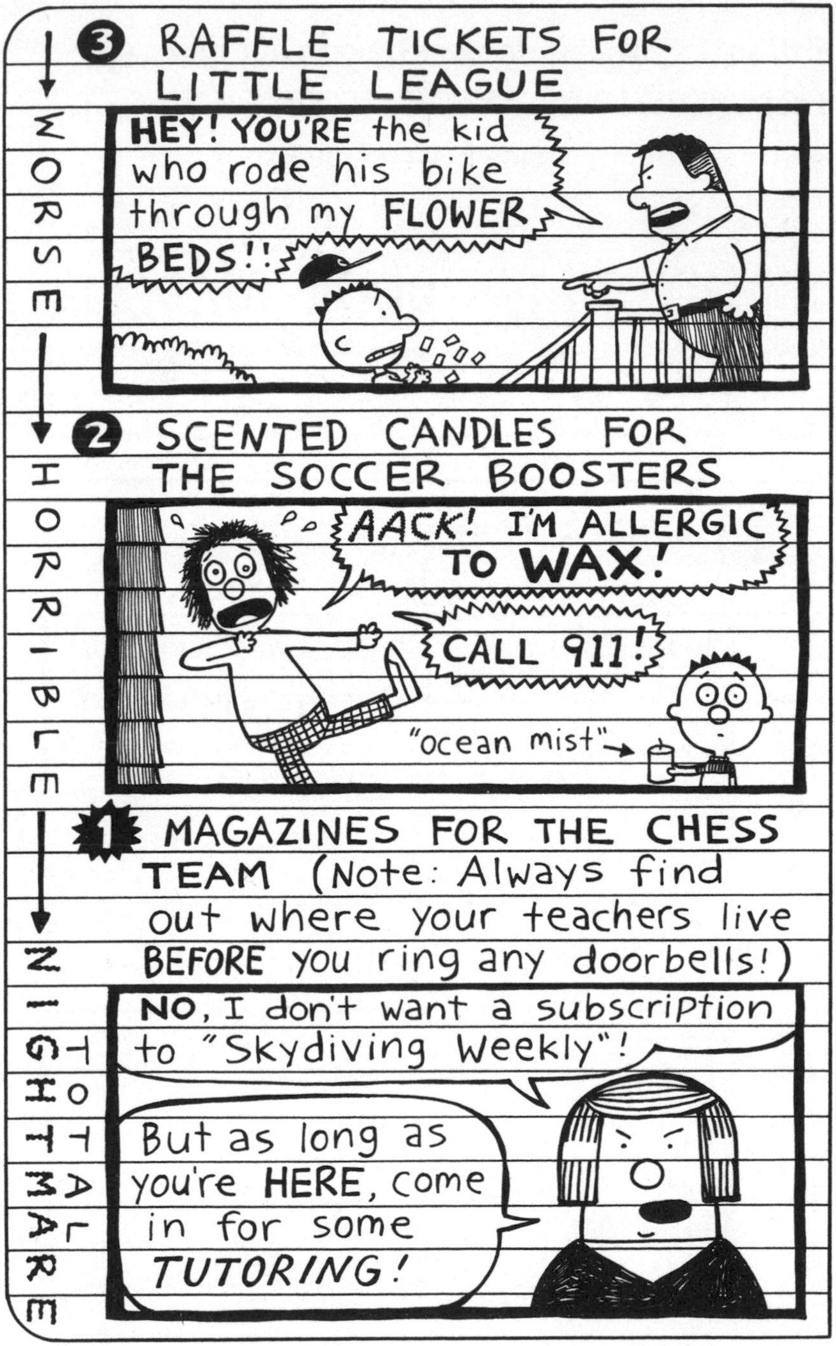
WORSE
3 RAFFLE TICKETS FOR LITTLE LEAGUE
HEY! YOU'RE the kid who rode his bike through my FLOWER BEDS!!
HORRIBLE
2 SCENTED CANDLES FOR THE SOCCER BOOSTERS
AACK! I'M ALLERGIC TO WAX!
CALL 911!
"ocean mist"
TOTAL NIGHTMARE
1 MAGAZINES FOR THE CHESS TEAM (Note: Always find out where your teachers live BEFORE you ring any doorbells!)
NO, I don't want a subscription to "Skydiving Weekly"!
But as long as you're HERE, come in for some TUTORING!

"How come we have to do a fund-raiser, anyway?"
I grumble.

"That's just for the cost of our uniforms," explains
Francis. "We need extra money to upgrade our
camping gear."

I snort. "We won't raise much selling THIS junk."

Francis frowns. "You'll need a better sales pitch than THAT," he says, "if you want to win one of the prizes."

"There's a first, second, and third place prize for the scouts who sell the most wall hangings," he explains patiently. "And they're GOOD prizes, too, because this fund-raiser isn't just for OUR troop! . . ."

Francis jumps. "My alarm!" he says.

"Wait! Francis! What are the prizes?"

"They're on the back of the brochure I gave you!"
he calls over his shoulder. "I'll see you later!"

I flip the brochure over.

A build-your-own-
robot kit? Not really
my thing, unless the
robot can do my
social studies home-
work for me.

No, thanks. Telescopes are a total rip-off. They're always like: "Explore the galaxy!" But when you actually look through them, all you can see is a reflection of your eyeball.

And the GRAND prize is . . .

A blast of energy shoots through me. Suddenly, selling those lame wall hangings seems a lot more interesting. Now there's a GOAL to work toward. Now I'm MOTIVATED.

For a prize like THIS, I'll sell ANYTHING!

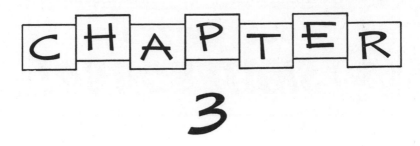

CHAPTER 3

"Prepare to finish second, guys!" I announce the next morning when I meet Francis and Teddy for the walk to school.

"Wait a minute," says Francis. "Yesterday all you could talk about was how LAME those things were!"

"They ARE lame," I say.

Francis gives me one of his looks. "Uh, and what's the 'Nate Wright charm,' exactly?"

"That's a question MANY have asked," Teddy says.

"You clowns wouldn't know charm if it hit you on the head," I say.

Which, come to think of it, sounds like a pretty good idea!

"Hey, it isn't me or Teddy you have to worry about," says Francis.

"Artur?" I repeat. "What do you mean?"

"He seemed pretty psyched about the fund-raiser at our meeting yesterday," Francis explains.

"Yeah," agrees Teddy. "He really wants to win that skateboard."

Skateboard? MY skateboard??

"I bet Artur's a good salesman," Francis says.

Great. I can picture it now.

Maybe I'm exaggerating, but not by much. Grown-ups tend to get all gushy whenever Artur's around, and I'll tell you why: He's always sucking up to them.

See? Artur's all deep in conversation with Mr. Galvin, who's not exactly Captain Charisma. Why would anyone talk to Mr. Galvin if they didn't HAVE to? Artur's the biggest suck-up in P.S. 38.

Correction: Artur's the SECOND biggest suck-up in P.S. 38. GINA's ahead of him.

Here's what bugs me: It WORKS. The sucking up, I mean. The teachers fall for it every time. They're always like: Artur's so THIS. Gina's so THAT. Artur and Gina. Gina and Artur.

Wait. Whoa. WOW!

I just got such a great idea, it almost blew my pants off!

Why didn't I think of it BEFORE? The two of them are so alike. They're king and queen of the honor roll, they never get in trouble, and they're both a total pain in my butt. So what are we WAITING for? Let's get these two lovebirds TOGETHER!

There's only one teensy little problem:

Artur's already going out with Jenny.

Don't ask me why. Everybody with half a brain knows that I'D be a much better match for Jenny than Artur. When you do a comparison, it's not even CLOSE.

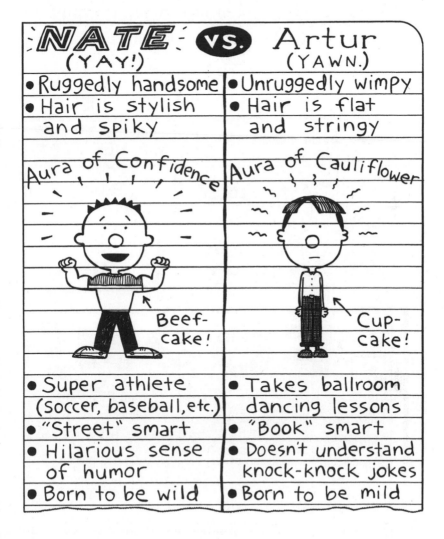

NATE (YAY!)	**VS.**	Artur (YAWN.)
• Ruggedly handsome		• Unruggedly wimpy
• Hair is stylish and spiky		• Hair is flat and stringy
Aura of Confidence		Aura of Cauliflower
Beef-cake!		Cup-cake!
• Super athlete (soccer, baseball, etc.)		• Takes ballroom dancing lessons
• "Street" smart		• "Book" smart
• Hilarious sense of humor		• Doesn't understand knock-knock jokes
• Born to be wild		• Born to be mild

Plus, I've known Jenny WAY longer than ARTUR has. She was just about to start liking me, and then HE had to move to town. It's an OUTRAGE!

But back to my brilliant idea: What if I can convince Artur that he and Gina are soul mates? Then he'll dump Jenny . . .

Oof. Pancaked by my own locker. That's a little embarrassing. Good thing Jenny's not around to see this.

"Nate," says a voice.

Oh, really? Thanks for pointing that out, Artur. That's so OBSERVANT of you!

I shove every-
thing back in
place and make
it to homeroom
on time. That's
key, because I

can't afford to get detention. Not today. I need to
be free after school . . .

. . . TO START SELLING **WARM FUZZIES!**

Allow **ME** to assist you!

BING!

So I turn myself
into Johnny B. Good
Behavior. When Mrs
Godfrey needs a
volunteer, I raise
my hand. When
Ms. Clarke asks a
question, I answer.

When Mr. Staples tells one of his lame jokes, I laugh. Basically, I spend the whole day acting just like Artur.

I hate myself.

But it works. I make

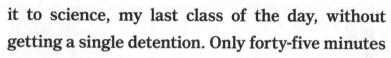

it to science, my last class of the day, without getting a single detention. Only forty-five minutes to go.

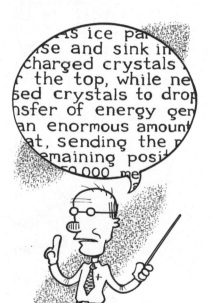

Mr. Galvin launches into one of his drone-athons, and I can feel my brain switch to autopilot. I can't stop thinking about that grand prize skateboard. It's WAY nicer than the one I lost in the creek.

I bet it's worth ten times as much. And it's CUSTOMIZED!

I hear something behind me. I turn around, and there's Gina peering over my shoulder. I slam the notebook shut,

but it's too late. She shoots her hand into the air in triumph.

I stare at Gina in disbelief. But why am I surprised? This is what she lives for. She shoots me an evil little grin.

"Bring me your notebook, Nate," Mr. Galvin says.

Young man. When they call you young man, it's pretty much a guarantee that you're getting detention. Unless you come up with a miracle. Unless you try something completely crazy.

Like the truth.

"Just a moment," Mr. Galvin cuts in. He gets up from his desk.

I swallow hard. How could telling the truth make things WORSE? Everybody's staring and whispering as I follow Mr. Galvin out of the classroom. The sound of the closing door echoes down the hallway. What's he going to do to me?

For the longest time, he doesn't do ANYthing. My ears are burning. My palms are slick with sweat. Finally, he clears his throat.

"Young man," Mr. Galvin says seriously, "you and I are going to have a little talk . . ."

CHAPTER 4

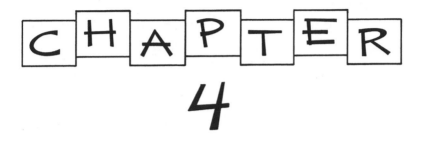

"You DID say you're a scout, didn't you?"

Where's he going with this? "Uh-huh," I answer nervously. "A Timber Scout."

"Yes sir," I say quickly.

"I'm going to let you in on a little secret, Nate," Mr. Galvin says. Wait, is he . . . SMILING?? Old Fossil Face NEVER smiles. Or maybe his dentures are slipping again. Either way, it's kind of creepy.

Whoops. I probably shouldn't have sounded so shocked. But it's sort of hard to believe that Mr. Galvin was ever a scout. Or a kid.

"We had to raise money back in MY day, too," he continues.

Believe it? Dude, I don't even know what a galosh IS.

"Now listen, Nate," he says, and suddenly he's Joe Serious again. "I don't approve of drawing during class . . ."

Really? Wow, this is like one of those stupid TV movies, where all of a sudden I realize:

. . . and then he says:

But exactly three and a half seconds later . . .

Okay, so I guess this ISN'T like one of those TV movies after all. I'd better get back to my desk and pretend to look busy. The NICE Mr. Galvin just disappeared. Say hello to his evil twin.

The day ends with a bang: I tell Gina that I didn't get detention after all. HA!

And speaking of Gina . . . remember my idea? The one about Gina and Artur getting together?

"Ah!" says Artur. "Hallo, Nate!"

Yeah, hallo yourself. Enough small talk. "Listen, Artur, ol' buddy," I say.

"Eh?" says Artur. "What abouts her?"

"Well . . . she's pretty nice, don't you think?"

Artur looks confused. "Why are you say?" he asks.

Come on, Artur, WORK with me. I can't make you and Gina a couple with THAT attitude. "She's got a lot going for her," I tell him. "She's smart, she's . . . ummmm . . . let's see here . . . she's . . ."

Sorry. Had something stuck in my throat for a sec.

Artur nods. "Hmm," he says. "Yes, I thinks I know what you are try to say."

You DO? Wow, I must be more convincing than I thought! Could Artur actually FALL for this??

I'm about to seal the deal when . . .

Sailing? Excellent! If Artur's stuck on a BOAT some-where, he won't be doing any FUND-RAISING! I remember what Francis said this morning:

 Here's my chance to get a head start on him. I sprint home, change into my uniform, and grab what I need:

And then there's my secret weapon: I'm a Timber Scout! People can't resist a man in uniform. Who wouldn't want to help a bunch of scouts buy some new camping gear?

I just hope our next camping trip is better than the LAST one.

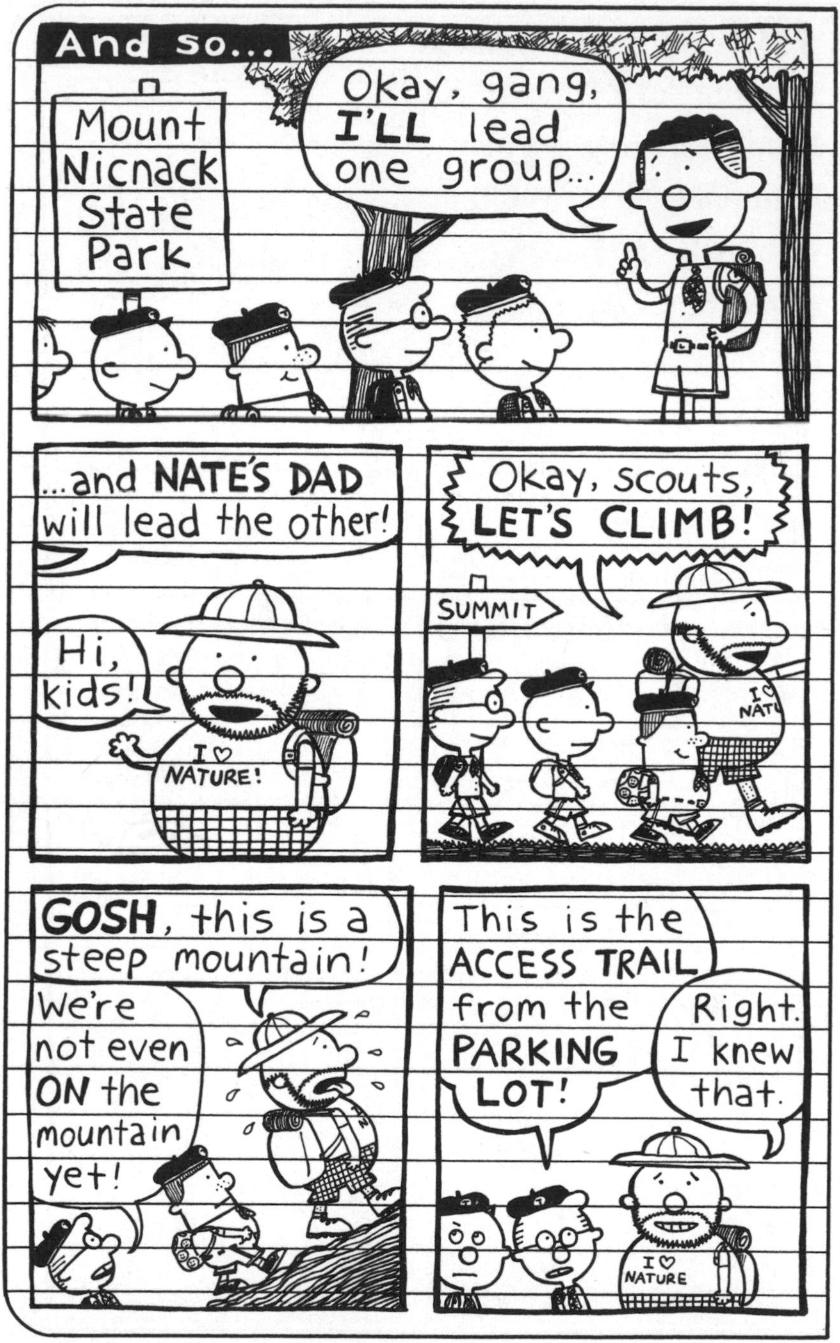
And so...
Mount Nicnack State Park
Okay, gang, I'LL lead one group...
...and NATE'S DAD will lead the other!
Hi, kids!
I ♡ NATURE!
Okay, scouts, LET'S CLIMB!
SUMMIT
GOSH, this is a steep mountain!
We're not even ON the mountain yet!
This is the ACCESS TRAIL from the PARKING LOT!
Right. I knew that.
I ♡ NATURE

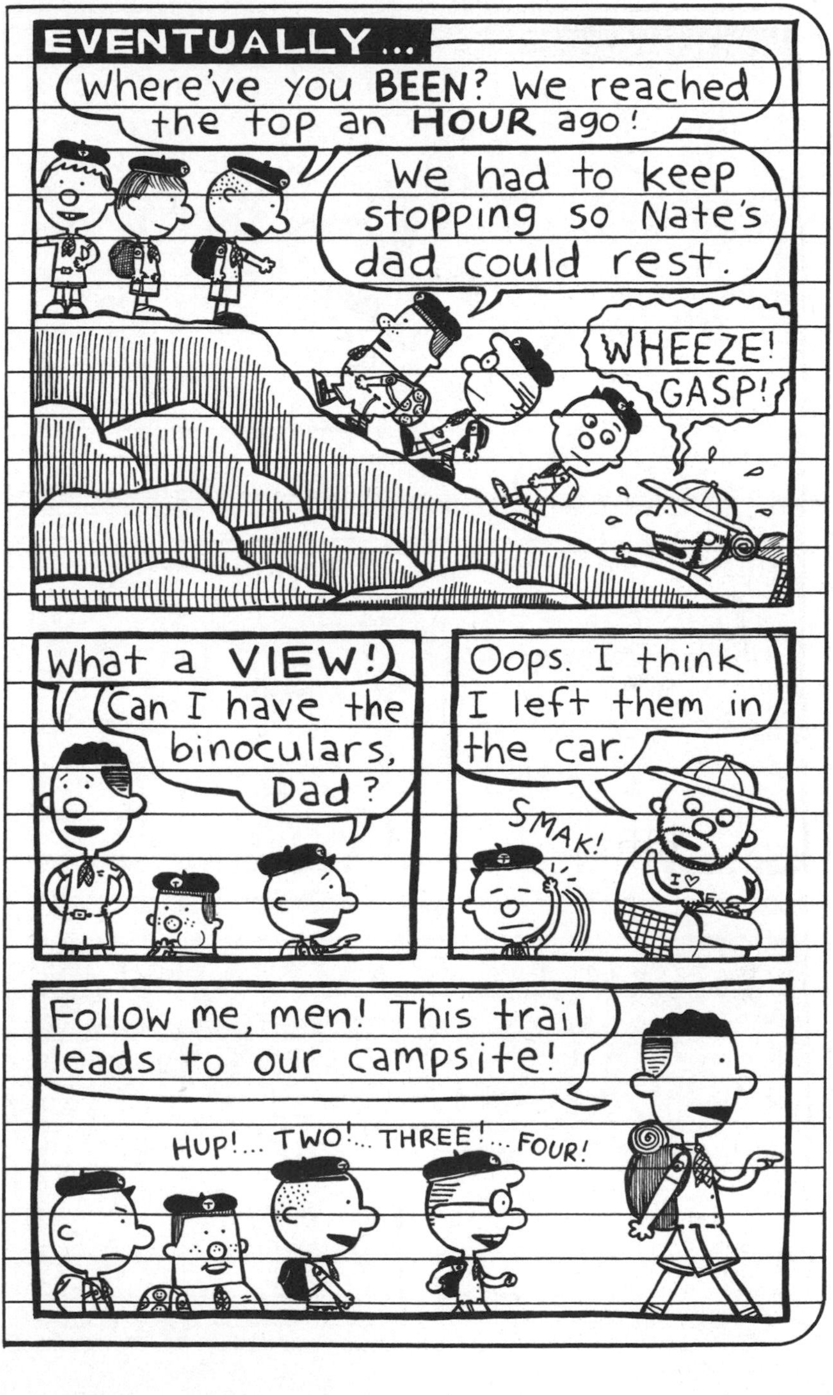

EVENTUALLY...
Where've you BEEN? We reached the top an HOUR ago!
We had to keep stopping so Nate's dad could rest.
WHEEZE! GASP!
What a VIEW!
Can I have the binoculars, Dad?
Oops. I think I left them in the car.
SMAK!
Follow me, men! This trail leads to our campsite!
HUP!... TWO!... THREE!... FOUR!

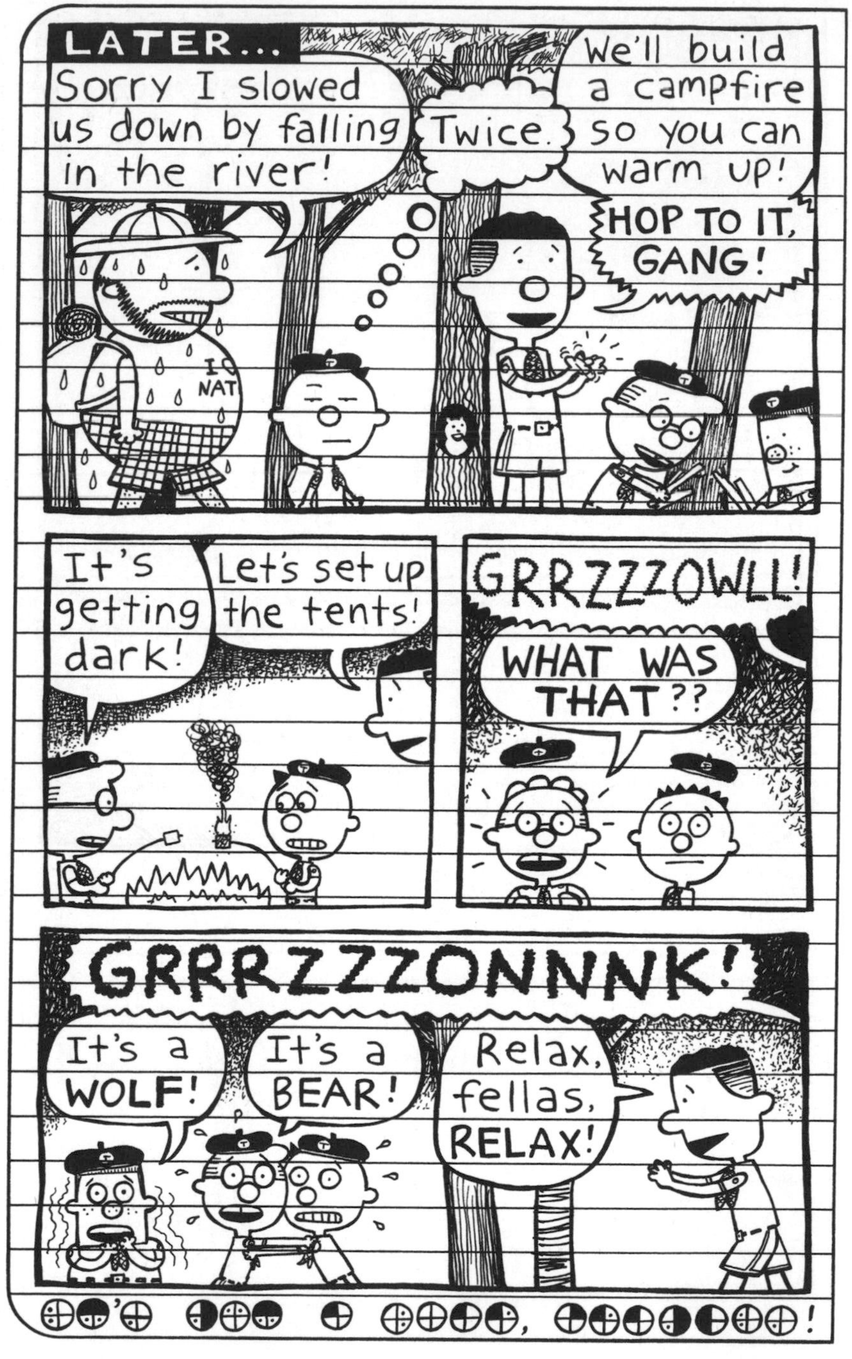
LATER...
Sorry I slowed us down by falling in the river!
Twice.
We'll build a campfire so you can warm up!
HOP TO IT, GANG!
I NAT
It's getting dark!
Let's set up the tents!
GRRZZZOWLL!
WHAT WAS THAT??
GRRRZZZONNNK!
It's a WOLF!
It's a BEAR!
Relax, fellas, RELAX!

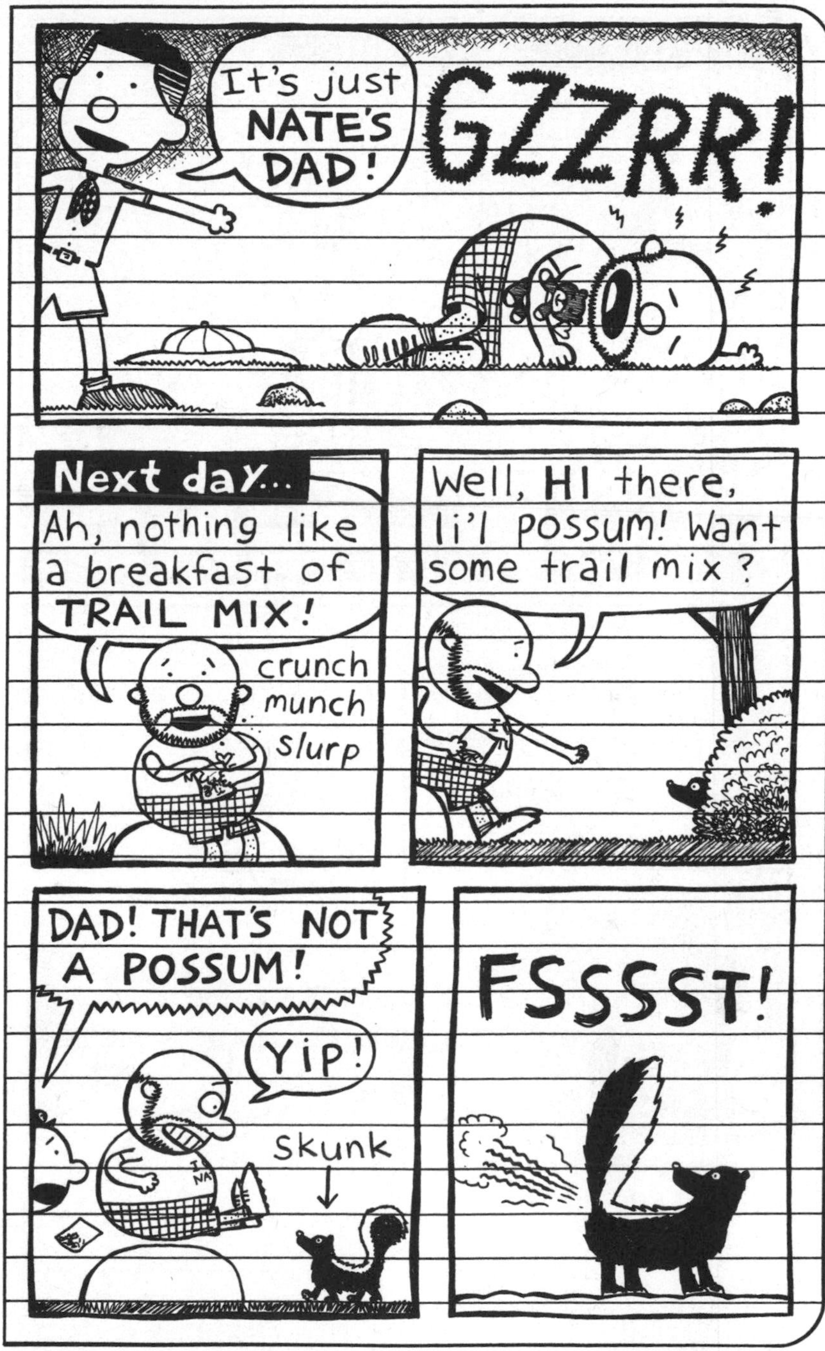

It's just NATE'S DAD!
GZZRR!
Next day...
Ah, nothing like a breakfast of TRAIL MIX!
crunch
munch
slurp
Well, HI there, li'l possum! Want some trail mix?
DAD! THAT'S NOT A POSSUM!
Yip!
Skunk
FSSSST!

And we all lived skunkily ever after. Or at least for the rest of that day. It takes a long time to get the stench off. After that, I made Dad promise never to be a parent volunteer again.

I head for Mr. Eustis's house. He probably THINKS he doesn't need one of these cheeseball wall hangings. But I'll convince him. Just wait 'til he hears my sales pitch.

SPITSY! NO! OFF! HEEL!

"Sorry about that, Nate," says Mr. Eustis, running over. "You know how much Spitsy likes you!"

Yeah? Well, he also likes chasing trees and licking himself for hours at a time. So excuse me if I'm not exactly flattered.

"Were you looking for me?" Mr. Eustis asks.

HUH?... OH! YEAH!

I'M RAISING MONEY FOR MY TIMBER SCOUT TROOP, AND...

Turns out, Mr. Eustis is a soft touch. Maybe it's because he feels bad that Spitsy used me as a tackling dummy, but he buys a wall hanging.

I write his name and address on my clipboard. That's eight bucks for the Timber Scouts. And more important . . .

After that it gets harder. For some reason, a lot of people aren't home at four o'clock. And the ones who ARE home have already bought stuff to support the track team, the Dungeons & Dragons Club, or the Left-Handed Needlepoint Society.

And some people are just flat-out weird.

But I plug away. After a couple of hours, I've sold five Warm Fuzzies. That's forty bucks!

I do some quick math. We've got a two-week selling period. If I sell five of these things every day for two weeks . . .

8 DOLLARS EACH...
70 × 8...
UMMMMMMM...

Did I mention how much I hate math?

The point is, if I can keep up this pace, I'll raise a ton of money for the Timber Scouts. AND I'll be WAY ahead of . . .

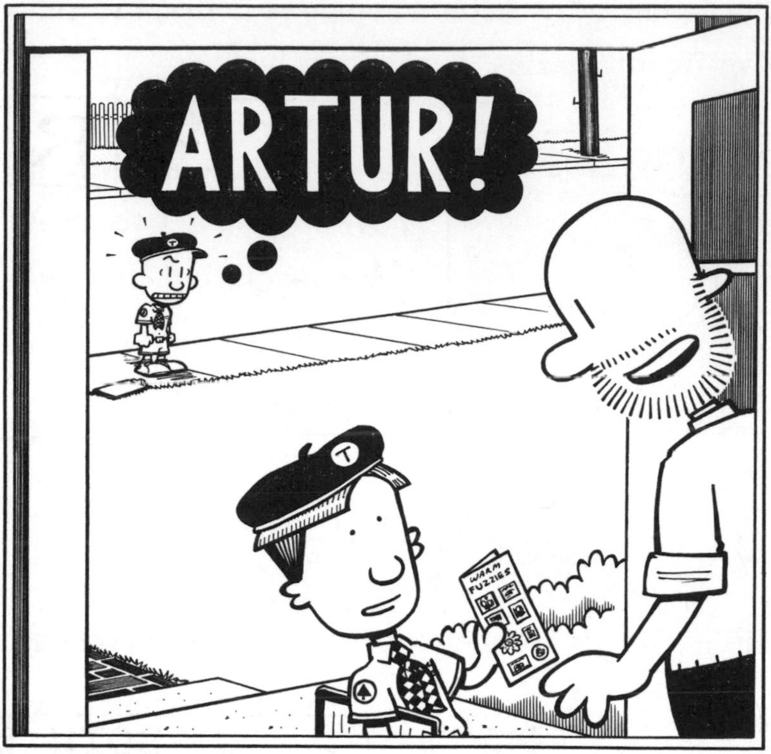
ARTUR!
WARM FUZZIES

CHAPTER 5

He sees me coming up the driveway. MY driveway.

Is he for real? What does he expect me to do—give him the Timber Scout secret handshake? Not that we HAVE a secret handshake. And by the way, what's he even DOING here?

He looks puzzled. "Yes, EXACT," he says. "Just like YOU, I am doing, Nate. Sailing wall hangings."

Sailing? SAILING??

"Ah!" he says. "Yes! SELLing."

Oh, brother. Here I was thinking Artur was cruising around on a LAKE somewhere, and he's been out selling Warm Fuzzies to my DAD! What a dirty trick.

"I am go home now," he says. "So longs, Nate."

"Wait just a sec, Artur."

I have to ask. I don't want to know, really. It's more like I NEED to know.

"Oh, not a lots," he says with a wave.

Twenty? Did he say TWENTY?? That's IMPOS-SIBLE! Nobody could sell twenty of those stupid wall hangings in two hours!

And then Dad walks up behind me.

I'll say this for the guy: His timing's incredible. Somehow, he always finds the very worst moment to make some amazingly boneheaded comment.

So here I am, ALREADY in a bad mood because his royal highness has sold FOUR TIMES the number of Warm Fuzzies that I have . . . and Dad drops this little bomb on me:

That does it. Tommy Tactless just pressed the wrong button. Stand back and cover your ears, everybody. I'm about to let Dad have it.

Except Dad's not done. "It was so thoughtful of him to bring those brownies," he says.

Huh? "Brownies?"

"He told me you missed out on the snack at your troop meeting yesterday," Dad explains.

I don't get it. "Didn't Artur try to sell you any wall hangings?" I ask.

"What? Of COURSE not," says Dad. He seems a little taken aback. "Why would he do that?"

I think about it. I guess Dad's right. Artur WOULDN'T do that.

Anyway, at least I don't have to yell at Dad now. Which is good, because if I yelled at him, he'd probably ground me.

Remember when I mentioned the school play? This year the Drama Club's doing "Peter Pan," and tonight is opening night. Francis, Teddy, and I are going together.

I'm pretty psyched to check it out, actually, because I've only seen "Peter Pan" once in my life. Dad took me and Ellen to some sort of community theater production. I was only in second grade, so some of the details are kind of sketchy. But here's what I remember about . . .

When the actors were flying around their bedroom, it was so **OBVIOUS** it was fake. **YOU COULD SEE THE WIRES!!**

I'LL **GET YOU, PETER PAN!**

According to the program, the guy playing Captain Hook was an expert clarinet player. So I'm guessing his hook wasn't real.

Ellen spent the whole night **LECTURING** me. Who died and made **HER** Miss Theater Authority?

It's called "**INTERMISSION**," not "**HALFTIME**."

POP CORN

I got a really bad gas bubble and had to go to the men's room. I was in there forever. So I totally missed a huge chunk of the play.

During the big sword fight scene, Captain Hook's sword snapped in half, which you could tell wasn't supposed to happen. So then somebody threw a new sword onstage, and Captain Hook caught it in midair and kept fighting. And then the crowd went wild, and Dad said:

An hour later I meet Francis and Teddy at our regular spot, and we head over to school.

"Good thing we bought our tickets in advance," Francis says.

" . . . have you guys sold any wall hangings yet?"

"Five," I say.

"Wow, I only sold ONE, and that was to my grand-mother!" says Francis. "Five's GOOD, Nate!"

"I know—isn't that sick?" I say. "Winning that skateboard is going to be harder than I thought."

"Well, if you don't win," Teddy points out, "at least you already have a nice board."

"Uh . . . not exactly," I say, and I tell them my horror story of the poodle, the bridge, and the skydiving skateboard. They react just how you'd expect your two best friends to react.

WA HA HA HA HA
OH HO
HO HO
HA HA

Francis pulls himself together. "Sorry," he says unconvincingly. "It really isn't funny."

"Not at all," Teddy agrees, chuckling.

"Then it's got something in common with YOU two morons," I say.

The cafetorium's already packed when we get there. "You guys go find us some seats," I tell Francis and Teddy. "I'll grab some programs."

What LUCK! She's ALONE! Artur, the amazing Velcro Boy, is nowhere in sight! I wonder if . . . HEY!

COULD MY PLAN BE **WORKING?**

Maybe my little talk with Artur about GINA is starting to sink in! Maybe he picked up the phone, called Jenny, and said:

Hallo. I am not take you to the play, because I am start to falling crazy in love with GINA!

Oh, Punkin!

GASP!

And if there IS trouble in paradise, I bet Jenny's really bummed out, right? She's going to need some cheering up . . . from Yours Truly!

Boy, what a buzzkill. Just as I'm about to say hi to Jenny, Mr. Wonderful swoops in with his diploma from charm school, flashing his sappy smile and wearing his scout uniform . . .

Wait a minute. Scout uniform?

Why is Artur wearing his uniform to the school play? That's just plain weird.

But there's no time to think about that now. They're dimming the lights. The play's starting.

And it's a good play, too. The only thing that goes wrong in Act One is when Michael (aka Chad) almost destroys the set during his flying scene. But frankly, that just makes it more entertaining.

Intermission comes along really fast. The lights go on, and we get up to stretch our legs.

"Let's get something to eat," Teddy says.

THEY'RE SELLING SNACKS IN THE LOBBY!

GOOD! I'M HAVING A CHEEZ DOODLE ATTACK!

We go out the door and around the corner. Suddenly Francis stops short.

"Guys!" he says, surprised. "Check THIS out!"

I stare across the crowded lobby. My stomach sinks into my socks. I can't believe what I'm seeing. Now I get it. Now I know why Artur wore his scout uniform tonight.

Forget about the snack.

I just lost my appetite.

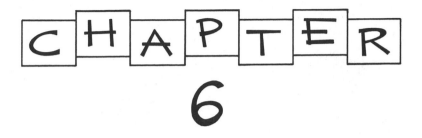

CHAPTER 6

The rest of the play is kind of a blur. I can't stop thinking about Artur.

Well, as long as I'm in a poetic mood, I might as
well go with it. How about THIS one:

Or maybe . . .

I write a few more poems about Artur in my head during the walk home. It helps me block out all the stuff Teddy and Francis are saying.

Okay, guys, I get it. Feel free to stop talking.

This really stinks out loud. Artur's been a Timber Scout for ONE DAY! How come HE gets to sell wall hangings at the play? Why does HE get special privileges?

Now he's even FURTHER ahead of me. He probably thinks he's won that skateboard already.

WELL, **THINK AGAIN**, AMIGO!

I am NOT going to roll over and let Artur beat me. I bet I can sell enough Warm Fuzzies to catch up to him. There's GOT to be a way!

FORTY-ONE...
FORTY-TWO...
FORTY-THREE...

And there it is! I mean, there SHE is.

Ellen has a part-time job at Daffy Burger. That explains why she's dressed like a ventriloquist's dummy. AND that pile of cash on the table.

"Have I got a deal for YOU!" I say, waving the brochure under her big ol' nose.

"I don't want to redecorate my room," she says flatly. "I like my room how it is."

Right. All those stuffed animals and teen idol posters? Classy, Ellen. Real classy.

I keep trying. Begging, actually. "It's for a great cause," I remind her. "Pleeeeeeeease?"

She gives one of those dramatic sighs. You'd think I just asked her to donate a kidney or something.

"Excellent choice," I say, even though the unicorn is the butt ugliest one there is. "And what else?"

Her eyes narrow. "ExCUSE me?" she says.

"I was . . . uh . . . hoping you'd buy more than one," I tell her. "Maybe three . . . or four . . ."

She snatches her money off the table. "Dream ON, Nate!" she snaps. "If you want to sell THAT many of your little wall hangings . . ."

Buy them myself. Gee, thanks, Ellen. That's about as helpful as a fart in a bathtub. That's . . . that's . . .

. . . BRILLIANT !

Let me rephrase that: I'M brilliant. My amazing brain just thought of a way to win that skateboard!

And I'll only have to sell those stupid Warm Fuzzies to one person:

ME!

Can you guess how I'm going to pull this off? Hang on while I grab a pencil and paper . . .

...AND I'LL EXPLAIN IT IN **WRITING!**

HOW I'LL BEAT ARTUR!

as explained by *PROFESSOR NATE*

Pay attention, class!

FACT #1: There is only ONE WAY to raise money for the Timber Scouts:

SELLING WALL HANGINGS!

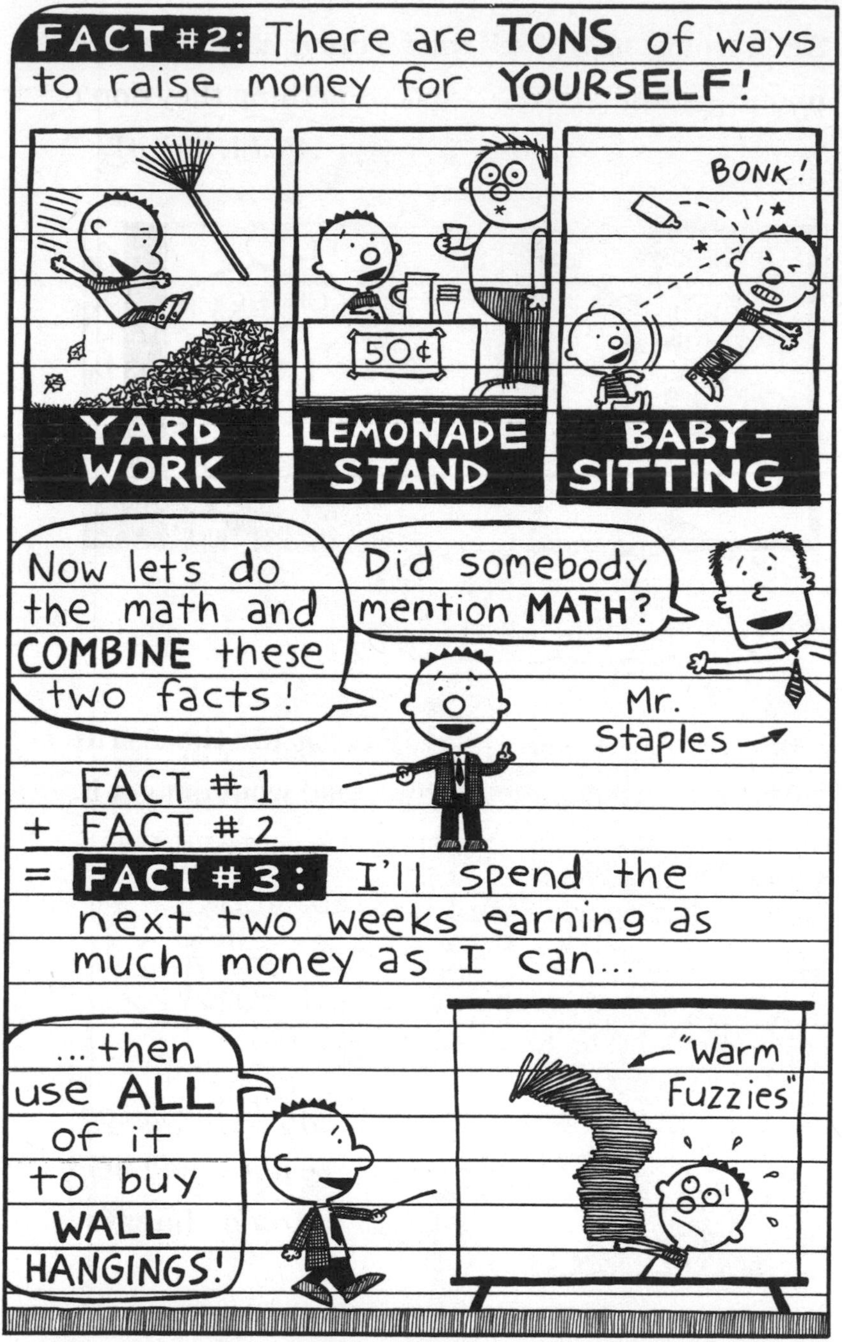
FACT #2: There are TONS of ways to raise money for YOURSELF!
YARD WORK
50¢
LEMONADE STAND
BONK!
BABY-SITTING
Now let's do the math and COMBINE these two facts!
Did somebody mention MATH?
Mr. Staples
FACT #1
+ FACT #2
= FACT #3: I'll spend the next two weeks earning as much money as I can...
... then use ALL of it to buy WALL HANGINGS!
"Warm Fuzzies"

See how it works? This way, I don't have to waste my time trying to sell people something they don't want! I can earn money however I FEEL like it!

"Did you have fun at the play?"

"Yeah, it was good," I say. Except for the Artur thing. But I don't mention that. Dad wouldn't get it.

"I'd be happy to buy a couple of these if it would help your scout troop," he says.

"Thanks, Dad, but you don't have to," I tell him.

NATE WRIGHT, *ACE BUSINESSMAN,* HAS GOT IT COVERED!

He gives me a look like he doesn't quite believe me. I'm used to that. When you're a genius like I am, it comes with the territory.

"Okay, well, good night, then," he says. "And don't stay up drawing comics, okay? It's late."

He's right, it IS pretty late. But I never go to sleep without drawing comics. It's part of my bedtime routine. It's like flossing, except it's more fun. And it doesn't make my gums bleed.

I'LL JUST DO A FEW PANELS OF...

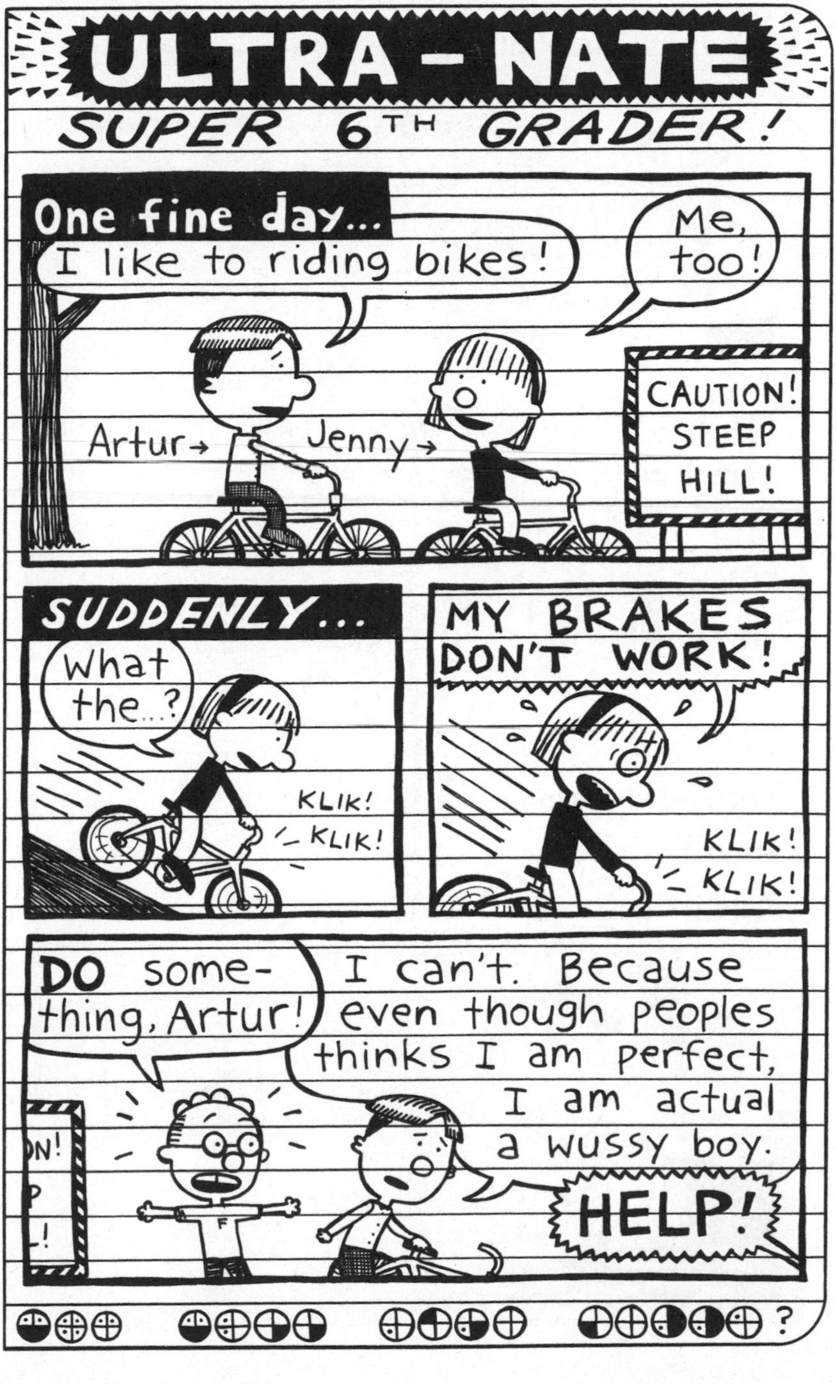
ULTRA-NATE
SUPER 6TH GRADER!
One fine day...
I like to riding bikes!
Me, too!
Artur→
Jenny→
CAUTION! STEEP HILL!
SUDDENLY...
What the...?
KLIK! KLIK!
MY BRAKES DON'T WORK!
KLIK! KLIK!
DO some-thing, Artur!
I can't. Because even though peoples thinks I am perfect, I am actual a wussy boy.
HELP!

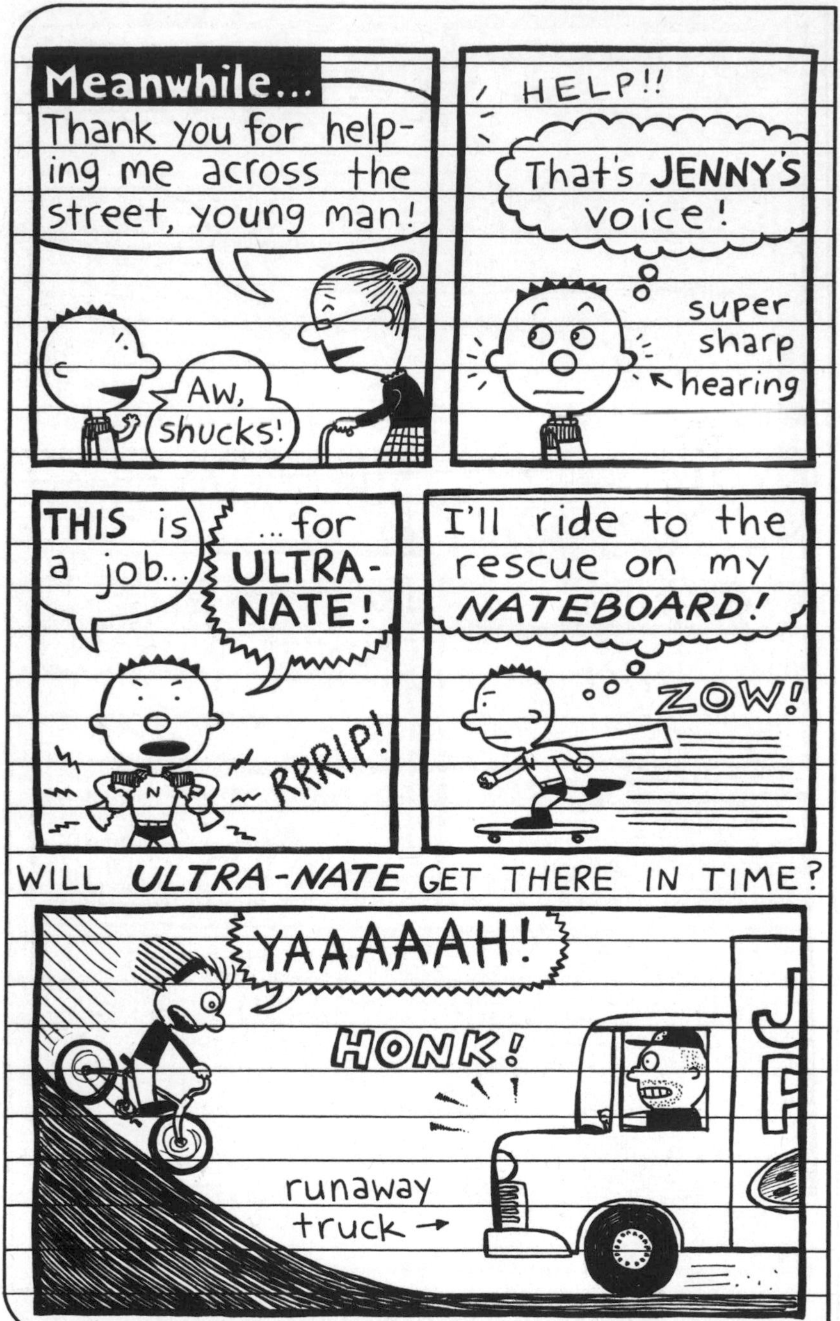
Meanwhile...
Thank you for helping me across the street, young man!
Aw, shucks!
HELP!!
That's JENNY'S voice!
super sharp hearing
THIS is a job...
...for ULTRA-NATE!
RRRIP!
I'll ride to the rescue on my NATEBOARD!
ZOW!
WILL ULTRA-NATE GET THERE IN TIME?
YAAAAAH!
HONK!
runaway truck

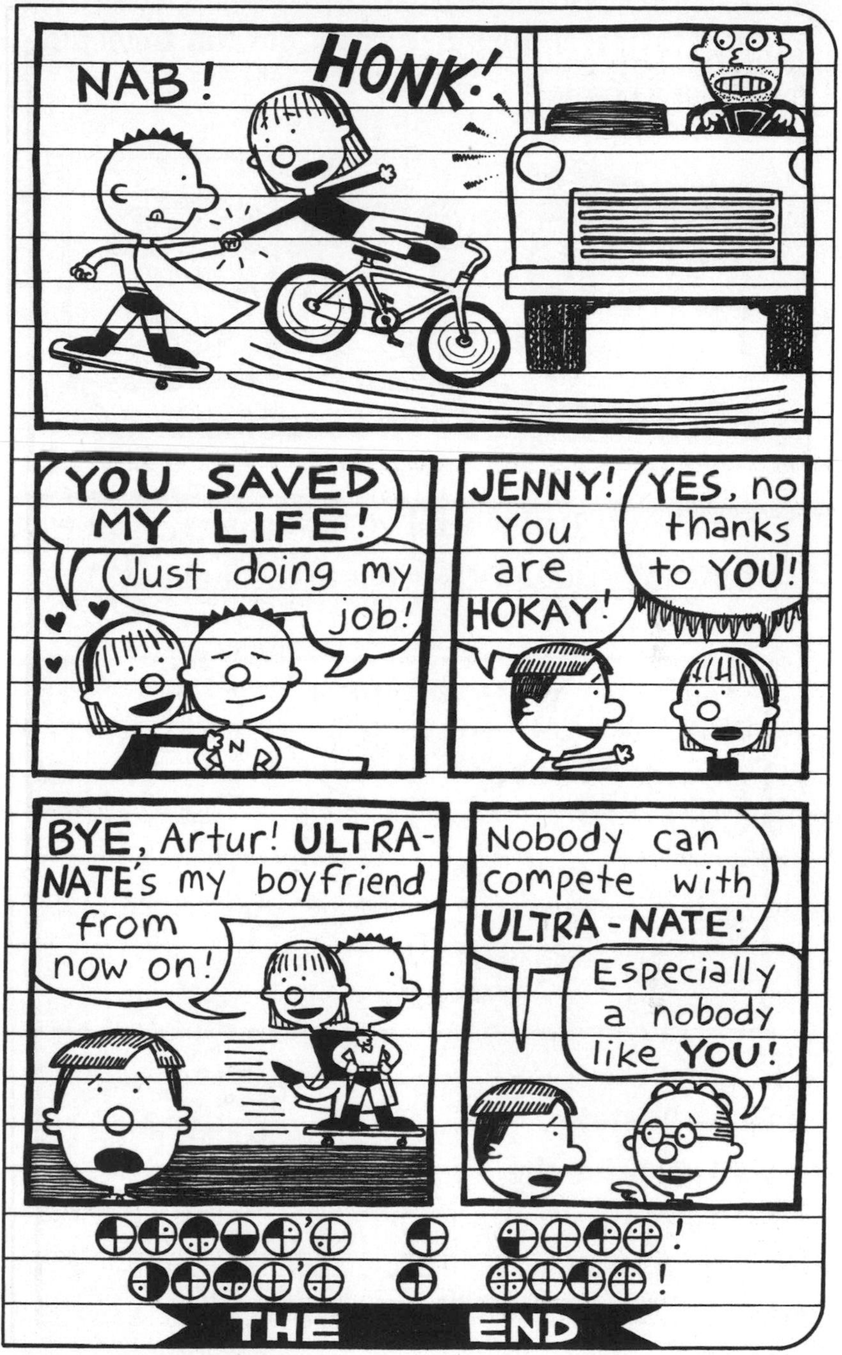
NAB!
HONK!
YOU SAVED MY LIFE!
Just doing my job!
JENNY! You are HOKAY!
YES, no thanks to YOU!
BYE, Artur! ULTRA-NATE's my boyfriend from now on!
Nobody can compete with ULTRA-NATE!
Especially a nobody like YOU!
THE END

The next morning's Saturday, but am I sleeping in? Not a chance.

"Nate," says Dad when I go downstairs, "will you please take these letters out to the mailbox?"

Oops. Mistake. Dad gives me the Hairy Eyeball.

"Never mind," I say quickly. "I'll do it for free."

"How generous of you," he says, still glaring at me as I scoot outside.

Okay, maybe I got a little greedy there. But how ELSE am I supposed to catch up with Artur? I've got to be on the lookout for any chance to make money.

"Oh, just a sprained knee," he says. "I've got to take it easy for a few days, that's all."

Hear that?  Opportunity is knocking!

"So you'll need someone to walk Spitsy!" I point out.

"That's right," he answers.

We make a deal: Mr. Eustis agrees to pay me eight dollars a day for walking Spitsy all week. That's enough to buy seven Warm Fuzzies!

"You can start right now," he says, handing me Spitsy's leash. "But be careful, Nate . . ."

"Don't worry, Mr. Eustis," I say confidently. "We're only walking to the park and back."

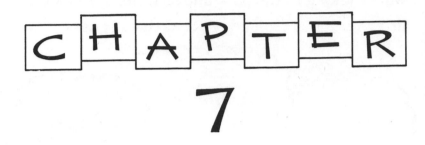

Everything. THAT'S what could go wrong . . .

I'm not just talking about walking Spitsy. The whole WEEKEND was a disaster. Sure, I made a little money, so I'm happy about that. I guess.

I thought dogs were supposed to have some sort of built-in GPS, but not Spitsy. He couldn't find his way out of a paper bag. And that's just ONE of the reasons he's a total failure as a dog. Here are a few others:

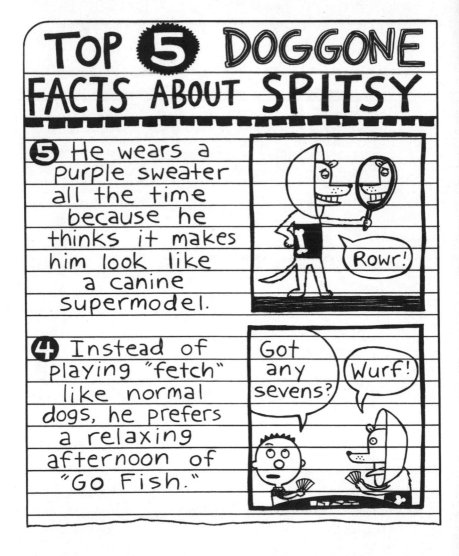

3 He gets bullied by the neighborhood squirrels.

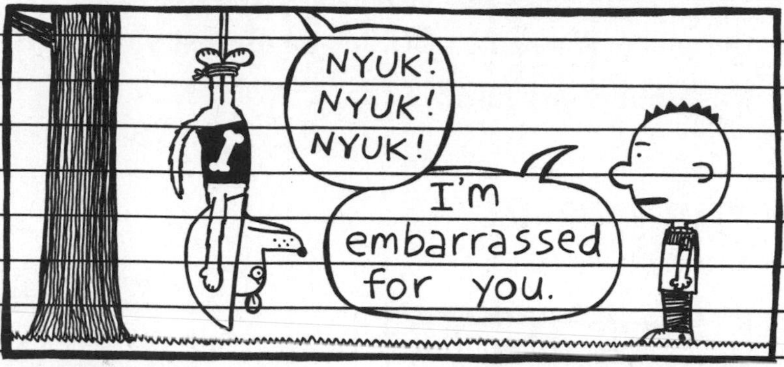
NYUK! NYUK! NYUK!
I'm embarrassed for you.

2 He comes over to our house all the time to watch lame TV shows with Ellen.

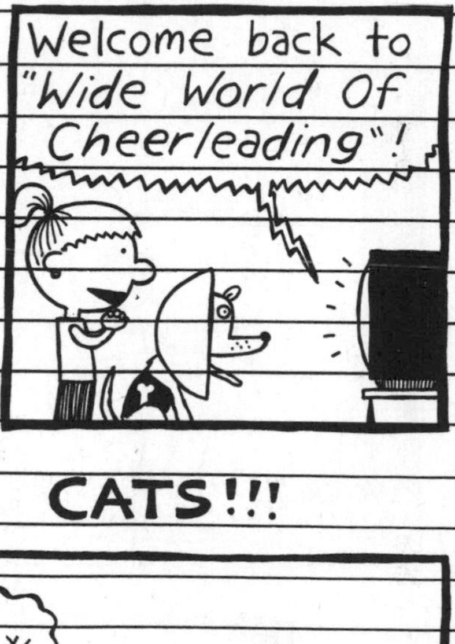
Welcome back to "*Wide World Of Cheerleading*"!

1 HE LIKES CATS!!!

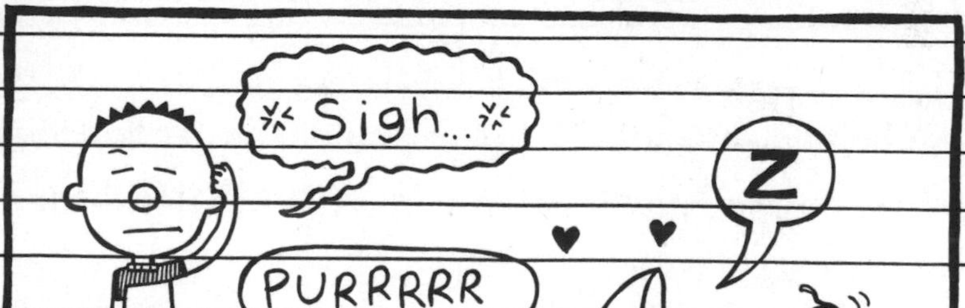
Sigh...
Z
PURRRRR

Anyway, I saw right away why Mr. Eustis called Spitsy unpredictable. He kept zigzagging all over the place. A couple of times he almost yanked the leash out of my hand.

So I tied it to my belt.

A belt-leash combo! It sure seemed like a good idea at the time. Maybe even a MONEYMAKING idea. There must be lots of dog owners out there who'd pay for a quality product like this.

Then Spitsy saw Pickles.

Pickles is Francis's cat. I'm no cat expert—I HATE cats—but I know there are two kinds: indoor and outdoor. Pickles is an outdoor cat. She acts like she owns the neighborhood, lying around in random driveways and giving everybody the evil eye. She's totally obnoxious.

You know what else she is? Spitsy's girlfriend. At least SPITSY thinks so. Whenever he sees her, look out. He goes from zero to crazy in no time flat.

He took off. And I was right behind him. With that leash tying us together like a couple of escaped convicts, I didn't exactly have a choice.

What is it with me and dog leashes lately? That one on the bridge cost me my skateboard. And THIS one nearly KILLED me.

Want some advice? Don't run into a tree at full speed. One of you is going to end up with a headache. And it won't be the tree.

Of course the leash came loose. Spitsy took off. And guess who had to spend an hour tracking down the happy couple.

And then, when I finally dragged Spitsy back home, I had to deal with Dad. Or, as I like to call him . . .

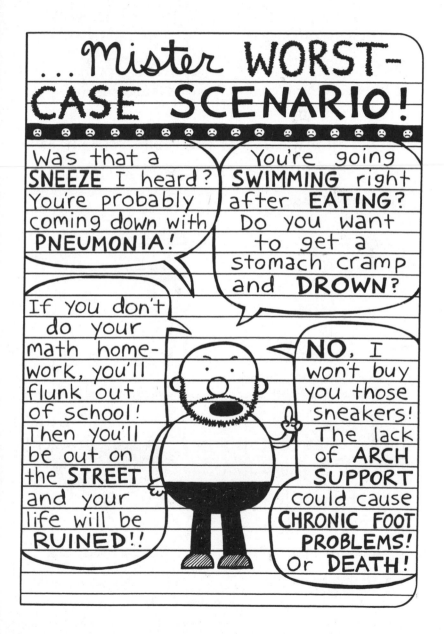

Dad overreacts to everything. So when he saw my

eye swelling up like a soccer ball, of course he was POSITIVE I had a concussion.

I didn't. But we wasted two hours going to the emergency room just so some doctor could shine a flashlight in my eyes and say:

Great. So instead of making money to keep up with Artur, I was stuck on the couch, holding a bag of frozen peas on my face. What a waste of a Saturday.

But I still had Sunday . . . AND a guaranteed fool-proof plan. I got up super early and spent an hour cranking out some eye-catching business cards.

Before anyone was awake, I went all over the neighborhood, sticking cards in doors and on windshields.

Then I went home and waited for the phone to ring.

AND IT DID!!!

Not just once. It rang OFF THE HOOK. Mrs. McNulty hired me to weed her garden. The Petersons asked me to move some boxes into their basement. And when Mr. Eustis saw my black eye—hello, guilt trip!—he paid me to paint the railing on his front steps.

By midafternoon, I'd already
earned almost FIFTY DOLLARS!
Business was booming.
Everything was going great.

And then . . .

It was that lady who just moved into the Nelsons'
old house.

"Yup!" I told her. "That's my business card!"

"Well, I have a job for you, if you're available."

131

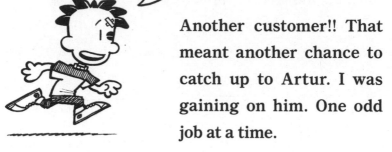

Another customer!! That meant another chance to catch up to Artur. I was gaining on him. One odd job at a time.

But this wasn't just an odd job.

This was BIZARRE.

At least two dozen ceramic lawn gnomes were grouped together by the porch. It looked like a coffee break at Santa's workshop.

"My friends and I need your help," the lady said.

Uh . . . friends? There was nobody else in the yard. Then I realized she was talking about the gnomes.

"Just move each gnome to the flag that matches his name," she instructed me cheerfully.

Yikes. It was already pretty weird that she had enough lawn gnomes to start her own football team. But she gave them NAMES? This lady was definitely a few slices short of a loaf.

"I'll pay you twenty-five dollars," she said as she went inside.

TWENTY - FIVE BUCKS !

That was good money. But it wasn't EASY money. Those gnomes were heavier than they looked. And, to be honest, they creeped me out a little bit. Maybe it was all those rosy cheeks. Maybe it was the stupid names like Cheeky, Krinkles, and Sir Potbelly. Whatever. I was halfway done when . . .

HI, NATE!

OH, HEY, KEVIN.

Kevin is Captain Hook in "Peter Pan." He was on his way to the show. And he had his sword with him.

"It's just wood with silver paint," he said, handing it to me. "Be careful with it—the handle's a little loose."

"Hey!" Kevin yelled. "Nate, LOOK OUT!"

I WAS looking out. I THOUGHT I was, anyway. The sword wasn't anywhere close to the gnome in front of me.

The gnome behind me wasn't quite so lucky.

Kevin grabbed the sword back from me and checked it for damage. "Are you DEAF or just STUPID?" he shouted angrily. "I TOLD you to be CAREFUL!"

He stalked off, shooting me a nasty look over his shoulder.

"SORRY, Kevin!" I called after him. "I guess I just . . ."

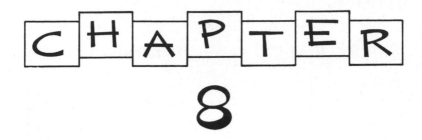

CHAPTER 8

"Well, this is a first," Francis says as we walk to school on Monday morning.

"What a tragedy," Teddy says. "For the gnome, I mean. Not for you."

"Oh yes it WAS tragic for me," I tell him.

Teddy cuts him off. "There ARE no interesting facts about lawn gnomes," he says. Then he points at a group of kids crowding around the bulletin board.

"Ooh!" Francis says, perking up. "They must have posted the Math Olympiad roster!"

There's actually something called the MATH OLYMPIAD? Sounds thrilling. What's next, a school punctuation team?

We elbow our way over to the bulletin board.

"So's Artur," notes Teddy.

"And so am I," says an obnoxiously familiar voice.

Oh, brother. Doesn't Gina ever get sick of patting herself on the back all the time?

"This is going to be SO much fun!" she exclaims.

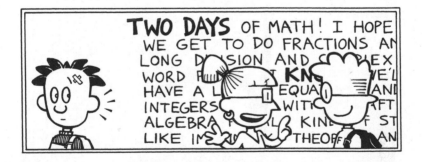

Huh? Two days? For the first time in her life, Gina just said something interesting.

"When IS this thing?" I ask.

"The Olympiad? This weekend," Gina says.

I don't even try to think of a snappy comeback. Did you hear that? THIS WEEKEND! That's PERFECT!

Francis chimes in. "It says here there'll be over FIVE HUNDRED kids competing!"

Normally, hearing about some humongous math meet would be about as interesting as watching Mrs. Godfrey bleach her mustache. But this is different. For TWO reasons:

See how it's all falling neatly into place? This is GREAT!

"Hallo, Nate," says a familiar voice.

"I hear you're going to the Math Olympiad this weekend, ol' pal!" I say, slapping him on the back. "You lucky duck!"

"Because you get to be teammates with GINA!" I say. "You two kids will be MAGIC together!"

Artur still looks confused. I'd better lay it on a little thicker.

"You know, I was Gina's partner last month for the social studies project," I say, putting a hand on Artur's shoulder.

"Nate," Artur says, "you are surprise me, the way you are talk about Gina."

Pretty smooth, right? Just call me Joe Cupid. If I keep planting these ideas in Artur's head, before long he and Gina will be on the express train to Togetherville.

And now, on to the next item on my list:

The whole odd jobs thing was okay, but it was a ton of work. And I obviously don't want a repeat of the lawn gnome fiasco.

Mrs. Godfrey looks mad—hey, THERE'S a surprise—and she's waving a piece of paper at me.

"This homework you handed in is COVERED with DOODLES!" she barks.

The idea hits me even before she's done talking.

I'll make my own comic book! That'll be WAY easier to sell than some stupid wall hanging. And here's the best part: Most of the work is DONE already! I draw comics ALL THE TIME!

For the rest of the day, I can't think about anything except my new business plan. At last bell, I don't wait for Francis and Teddy. I run home, zip up to my room, and start putting together . . .

It'll have old favorites, like this:

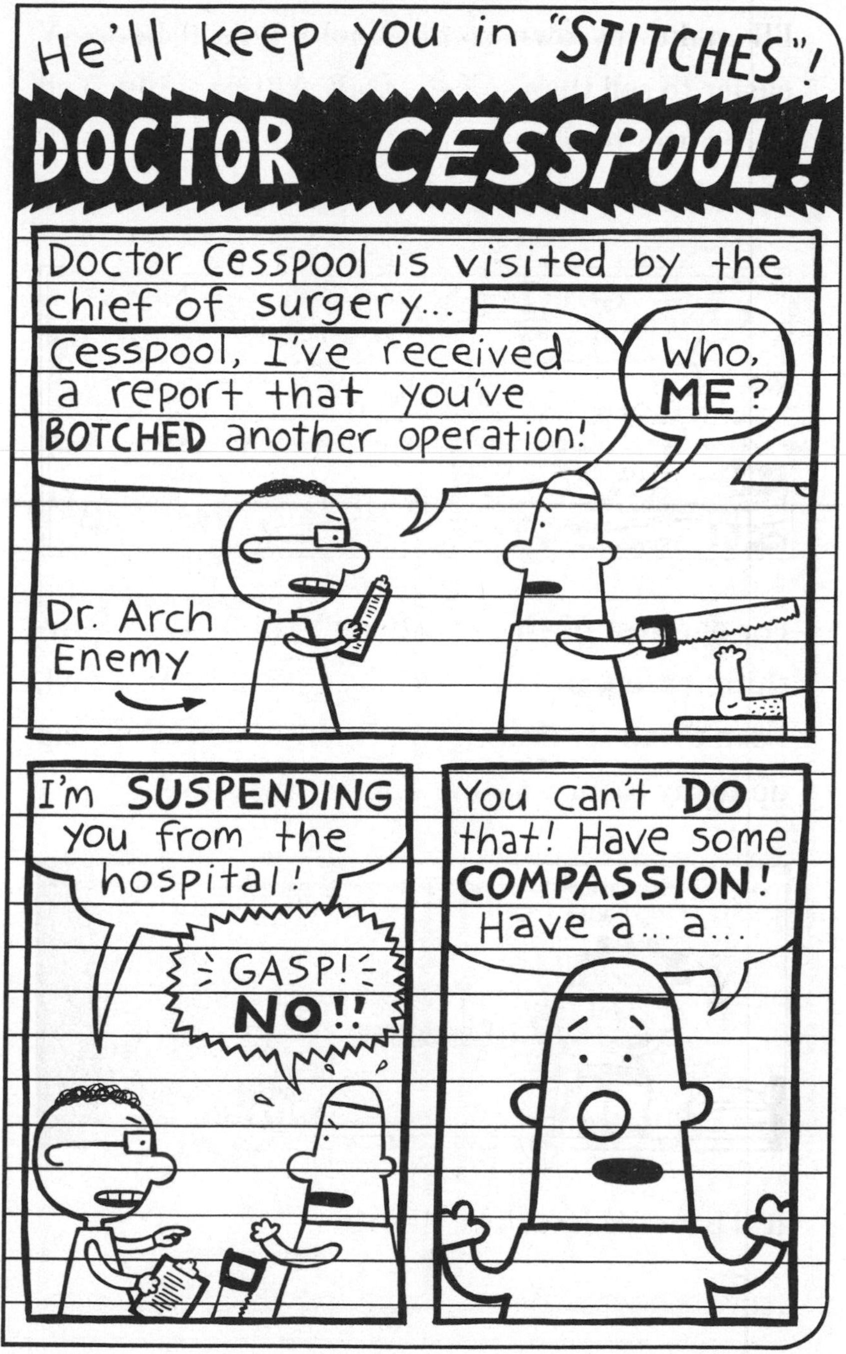
He'll keep you in "STITCHES"!
DOCTOR CESSPOOL!
Doctor Cesspool is visited by the chief of surgery...
Cesspool, I've received a report that you've BOTCHED another operation!
Who, ME?
Dr. Arch Enemy
I'm SUSPENDING you from the hospital!
GASP! NO!!
You can't DO that! Have some COMPASSION! Have a... a...

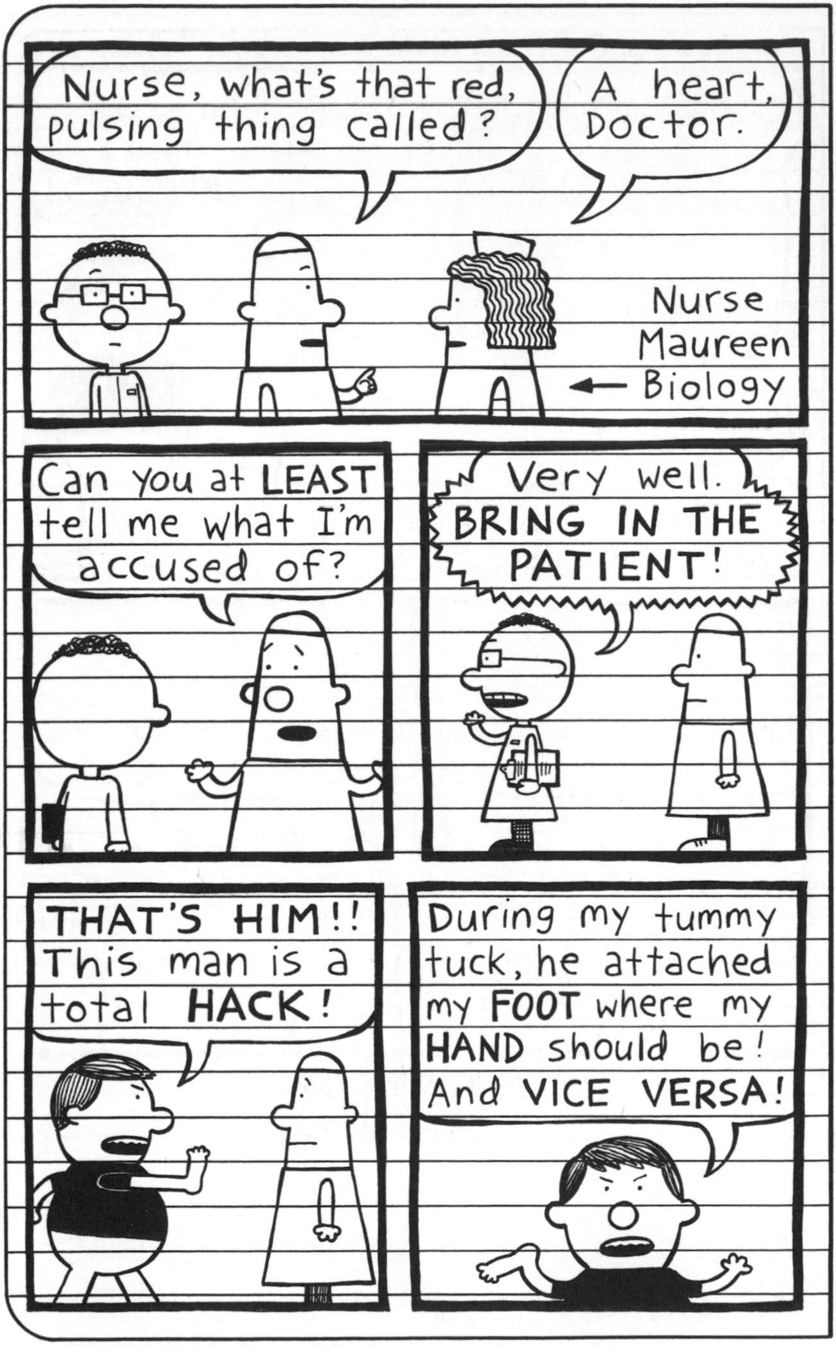

Nurse, what's that red, pulsing thing called?
A heart, Doctor.
Nurse Maureen ← Biology
Can you at LEAST tell me what I'm accused of?
Very well. BRING IN THE PATIENT!
THAT'S HIM!! This man is a total HACK!
During my tummy tuck, he attached my FOOT where my HAND should be! And VICE VERSA!

And I'll also sprinkle in some of my NEW creations, like this one:

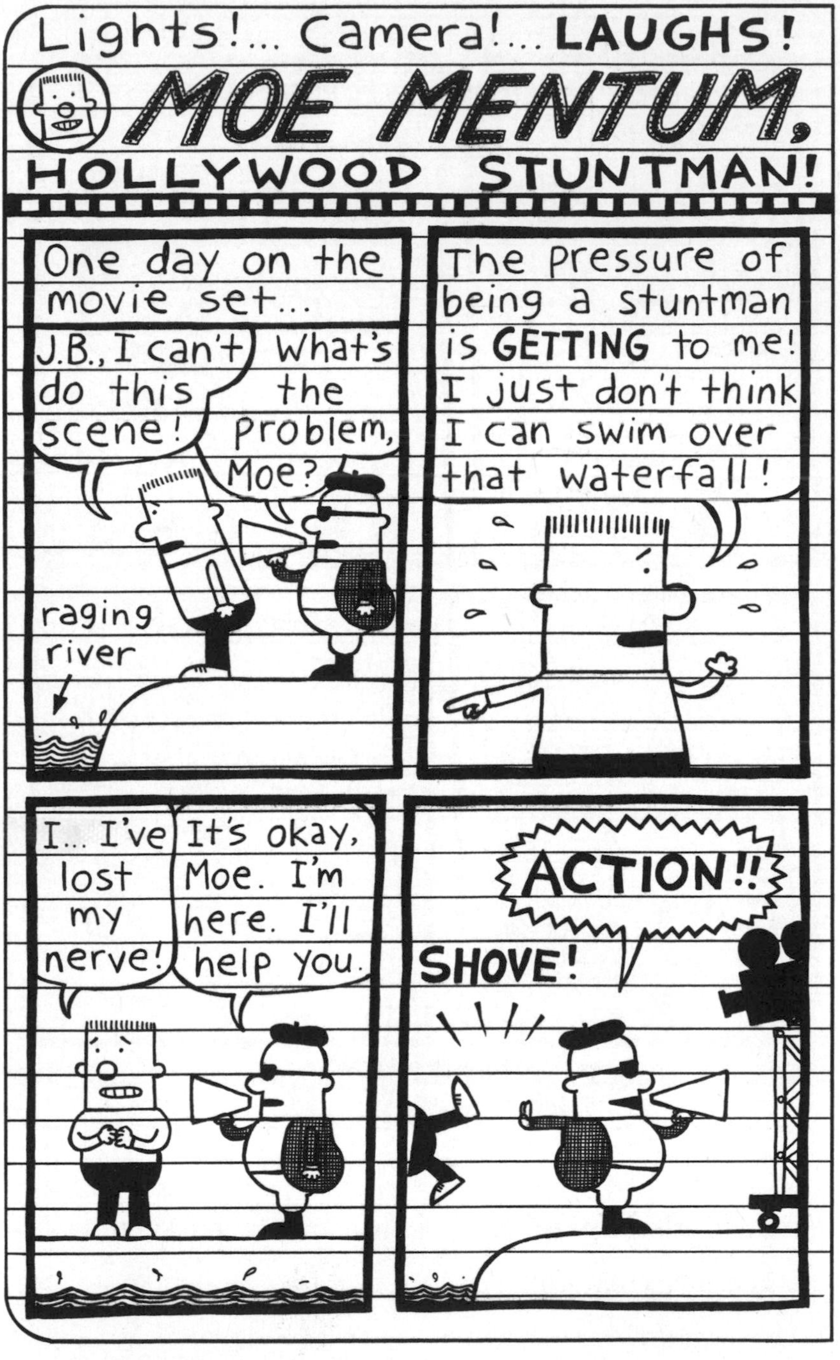
Lights!... Camera!... LAUGHS!
MOE MENTUM, HOLLYWOOD STUNTMAN!
One day on the movie set...
J.B., I can't do this scene!
What's the problem, Moe?
raging river
The pressure of being a stuntman is GETTING to me! I just don't think I can swim over that waterfall!
I... I've lost my nerve!
It's okay, Moe. I'm here. I'll help you.
ACTION!!
SHOVE!

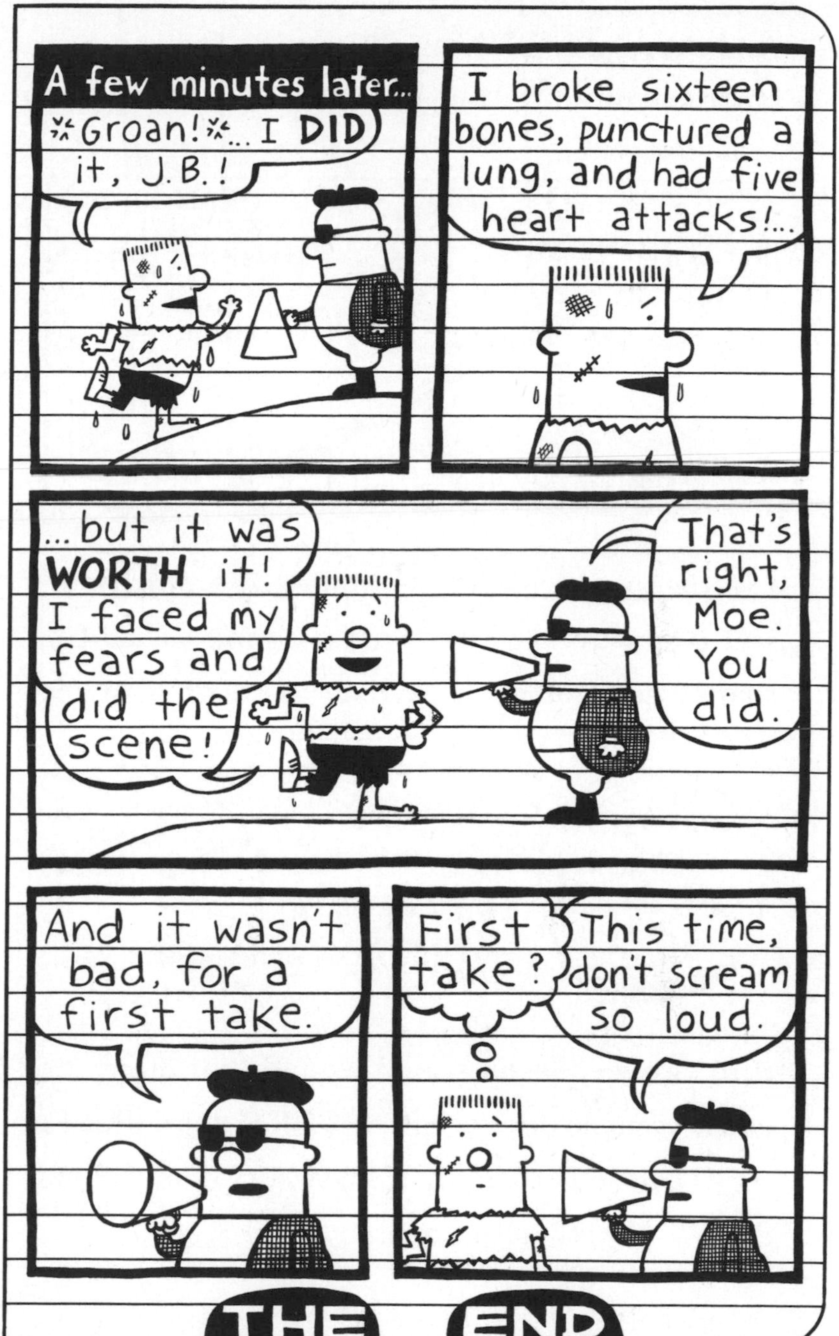
A few minutes later...
Groan!... I DID it, J.B.!
I broke sixteen bones, punctured a lung, and had five heart attacks!...
...but it was WORTH it! I faced my fears and did the scene!
That's right, Moe. You did.
And it wasn't bad, for a first take.
First take?
This time, don't scream so loud.
THE END

And that's only a few pages' worth. The complete book will be a LOT longer. The question is . . .

I settle on a nice, round number: five dollars. If I sell twenty copies of "Nate's Comix Crack-Up," that's a hundred bucks. Which is enough to buy . . .

Hm. Twelve doesn't sound like all that many. Not when you consider what ARTUR'S done. But I'm sure I can sell way more than twenty comic books. I'll just START with twenty.

"Um, yes, please," I say. "How much would it cost to make twenty copies of my comic book?"

She takes it from me, counts the pages, and punches the buttons on her calculator.

I practically pass out. That's almost as much as I earned this weekend! I gulp. For a few seconds,

I almost bag the whole idea.

Then I remember how awesome my comics are.

I pull a wrinkled wad of bills from my pocket and carefully count out thirty-four dollars. It seems like an awful lot of money. Still, I've heard people say that you've got to spend money to make money.

They'd better be right.

CHAPTER 9

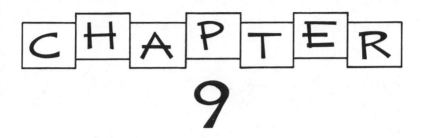

Unless you're one of those pencil necks going to the Olympiad, you're probably like me: You try to avoid math at all costs.

Here's what I mean: Since I spent all that money at the copy shop, selling twenty comic books for five bucks apiece doesn't equal a hundred dollars anymore.

That's only enough to buy EIGHT wall hangings, not twelve. I need to do better than that to catch Artur. Maybe I should sell them for six dollars instead. Or seven. But will people pay that much for a comic book?

Gordie has an after-school job at Klassic Komix in the mall. He's also Ellen's boyfriend. Dude. What were you THINKING?

But except for his putrid taste in girlfriends, Gordie's cool. And he's a total comics expert. If anybody can answer a comic book question, he can.

"We just got the new issue of 'Femme Fatality,' and it's INCREDIBLE!" he says. "I saved you a copy."

"Thanks, but I'm not buying today, Gordie," I tell him.

"It's my own original comic book," I announce.

He flips through it. "Mighty impressive," he says approvingly.

160

He kind of grimaces. "I'm not sure, Nate. That's pretty steep for a self-published book."

"But it's a RIOT!" I point out. "Can't we put it on display and let the CUSTOMERS decide?"

Gordie disappears into the back room while I stay by the counter. Then I notice a guy over in the corner. A big guy. A big, HAIRY guy.

He's talking to himself as he pulls some books off the shelves. Okay, that's a little weird.

He's putting stuff in his bag!

I turn to look for Gordie, but I don't have to. He's already here.

"SHOPLIFTER?" Gordie repeats. "Nate, he wasn't—"

"Yes, he WAS!" I shout. "He was STEALING stuff! I watched him do it! I'm an EYEWITNESS!"

Gordie holds up his hand like a stop sign. "Nate," he whispers, "that's Wayne."

Boss? HIM? The guy who made a wrong turn at one million B.C.?

"He was just getting rid of some stuff that hasn't been selling," Gordie says quietly.

Whoops. MAJOR whoops. But how was I supposed to know that? You've got to admit, the whole thing looked pretty suspicious.

"Uh . . . sorry about that, mister," I say.

Captain Caveman looks like he's getting in touch with his inner Godfrey. What's he gonna do, pull out a dinosaur bone and club me over the head?

(And, yes, I KNOW cavemen and dinosaurs weren't alive at the same time. It's an EXPRESSION.)

He fishes into his pocket and hands me a five.

"Here," he says. "I'll buy one . . ."

Oh, come ON. I can't walk around ringing door-bells again. That takes too long. There's got to be a better way to find . . .

DUH! Earth to Nate: You're standing in the middle of a MALL! This place is jam-packed with people looking to buy quality merchandise!

And quality's my middle name!

"But you've never seen a comic book like THIS one before!" I say, shoving it into her hand.

She turns to page one and frowns.

"Doctor CESSPOOL?" she says. "What kind of a name is that for a doctor?"

She hands the book back. "A man with a foot where his hand should be isn't funny," she sniffs.

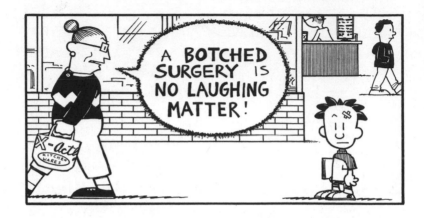

Wow. Speaking of surgery, can somebody give this lady a humor transplant? Lighten up, grandma.

I'll try Plan B.

"Check out this one!" I say, flipping the pages. "It's called 'Moe Mentum, Hollywood Stuntman!'"

The guy doesn't say anything; he just starts reading. I watch for a reaction.

Hel-LO? Is this dude even ALIVE? How could anybody read "Moe Mentum" without having some sort of . . .

Oops. Hold it. He's about to say something.

That's it? I offer him a chance to read a comic masterpiece, and all he can say is "I don't get it"?

There's a LOT that you don't get, pal. Exhibit A: You're wearing socks with your sandals. Which officially makes you a member of . . .

Obviously, my comics are too sophisticated for some people. Fine. Who needs 'em? There are plenty of other fish in the sea. I just need a way to reel 'em in.

That's IT! The perfect solution! Why talk to one customer at a time . . .

TESTING! 1...2...3... *TESTING!*

LISTEN UP, FOLKS! DO YOU LIKE **COMICS**? THEN GET YOUR BUTT OVER TO THE INFORMATION DESK AND BUY A COPY OF NATE'S **COMIX CRACK-UP!** NONSTOP LAUGHS! GUT-BUSTING GAGS! AND WHAT A **BARGAIN!** ONLY **SIX DOLLARS!!**

MAKE IT **SEVEN** AND GET YOUR COPY **AUTO-GRAPHED!!**

* AHEM! *

!

Uh-oh. Mall cop.

"What are you trying to pull, junior?" he asks angrily. He's breathing hard. He must have run all the way over here from the food court.

"Kid, you can't just walk in off the street and SELL stuff!" he sputters. "Not unless it's for some charity or school or—"

IF YOU WERE A **TIMBER SCOUT**...

...YOU'D BE WEARING A **UNIFORM!**

Gulp. Officer Friendly's got a point. And he's just getting started. He spends the next fifteen minutes going over all the important mall rules I've broken.

Finally, lecture time's over. He hands me a cell phone. "Call a parent to come get you."

For a second, I consider telling him I don't HAVE a parent. Being an orphan doesn't sound so bad right about now.

beep boop boop beep boop beep boop

BUT I GUESS I HAVE NO CHOICE!

BRRINNNG!

Don't pick up, Dad. Don't pick up. Don't . . .

"Hello?"

"Uh . . . hi, Dad, it's me," I say.

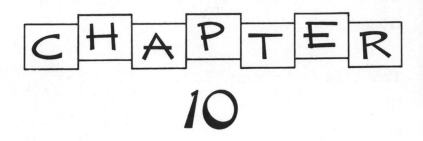

CHAPTER 10

Ever been grounded?

It does in MY family, anyway. I know kids who get in trouble and they're all: "Ooh, my parents

GROUNDED me." But, EXCUSE me, they're still watching TV, talking on the phone, and using the computer. They can still DO stuff.

That's not how it is in OUR house. When Dad grounds me (notice I said "me" and not "us," because Ellen's NEVER been grounded), he  doesn't mess around. There's no TV. No phone. No computer.

Dad doesn't see it that way. He says being grounded is an "opportunity." To do what—rearrange my sock drawer? I guess when you're Dad's age, sitting in your bedroom and slowly going bald is what passes for excitement. According to him, there's PLENTY to do when you're grounded.

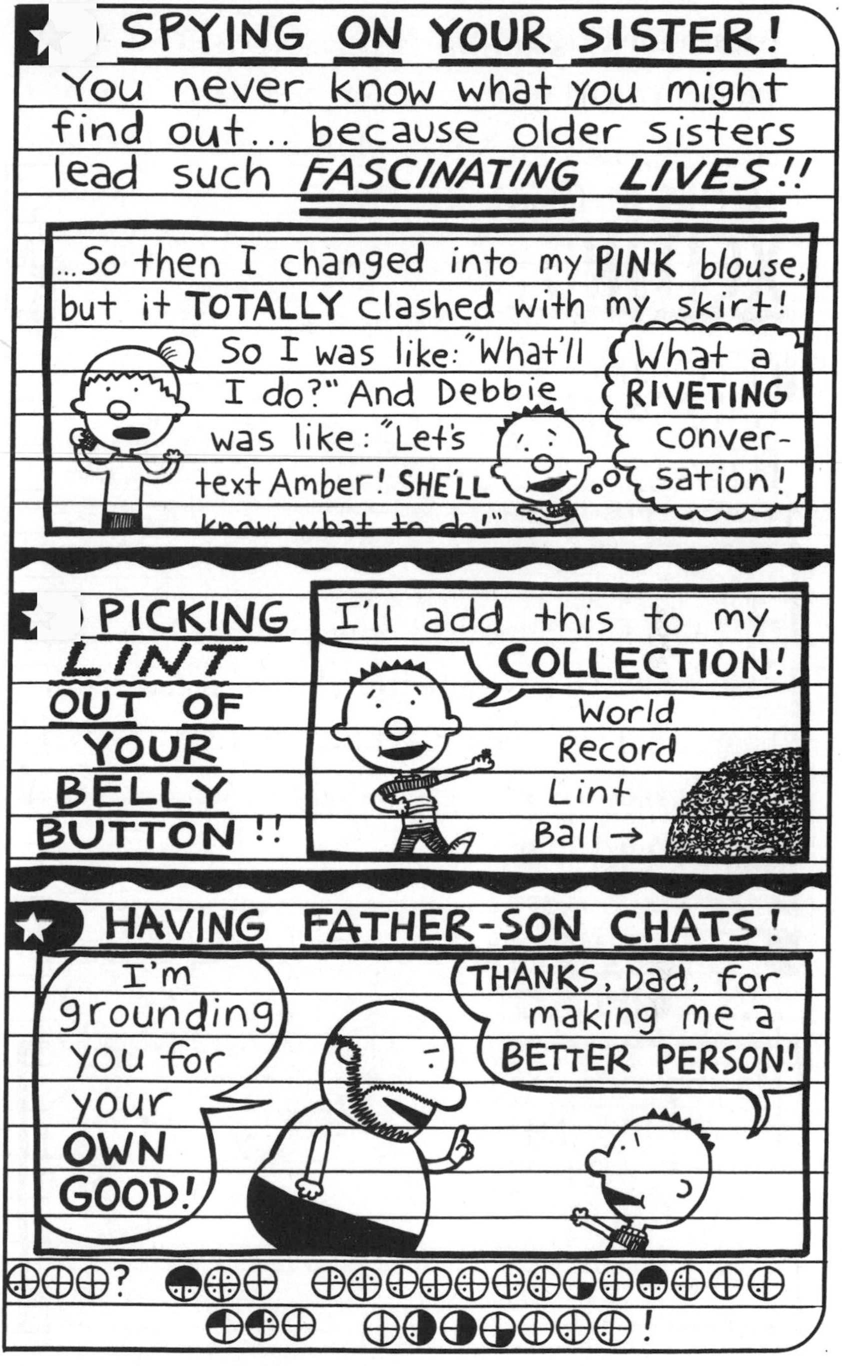

SPYING ON YOUR SISTER!
You never know what you might find out... because older sisters lead such FASCINATING LIVES!!
...So then I changed into my PINK blouse, but it TOTALLY clashed with my skirt!
So I was like: "What'll I do?" And Debbie was like: "Let's text Amber! SHE'LL
What a RIVETING conversation!
PICKING LINT OUT OF YOUR BELLY BUTTON!!
I'll add this to my COLLECTION!
World Record Lint Ball →
HAVING FATHER-SON CHATS!
I'm grounding you for your OWN GOOD!
THANKS, Dad, for making me a BETTER PERSON!
? !

Sounds fun, right? And being stuck here means I can't earn any money, either. So I haven't gained on Artur at all—not even while he was at that stupid Math Olympiad.

If Danny Discipline had only grounded me for a day or two, I'd have a better chance at that skateboard. But it's been a WEEK already! The only other time I've been grounded this long was that day I shaved Spitsy.

I still don't know what I did wrong. I mean, how ELSE was I going to get all that superglue off him?

Dad turns all serious on me when I come to the table. "Nate," he says, "provided you make it through school today with no INCIDENTS . . ."

YES! I'm FREE! Or I will be once school is over. I slam down my breakfast, brush my teeth, and grab my backpack.

Oops. I just remembered: Francis and Teddy went to school early this morning for BBC.

That stands for Breakfast Book Club. Hickey—Mrs. Hickson, the librarian—has BBC meetings every other Tuesday. Kids come in early to talk about whatever books they're reading, and Hickey serves apple juice and donut holes.

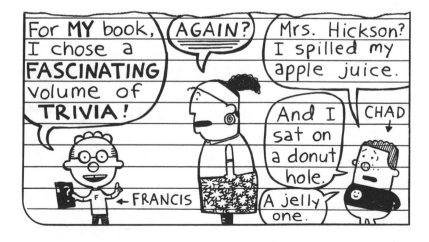

I'd be at BBC, too, if Dad hadn't thrown me in solitary. I wonder what I'm missing. I bet Amanda Kornblatt is talking about another horse book. If it doesn't say "pony" in the title, she . . .

Huh? Did they just say my name?

Okay, what's going on? Why's everyone talking about me? It can't be because of my little mall cop episode. That's old news by now.

I spot Teddy and Francis leaving the library. Forget telling them that I'm not grounded anymore; now I just want to ask them . . .

I'm getting annoyed. "What's so FUNNY?"

Say WHAT? LOVE BUNNY?? What am I—one of Ellen's stuffed animals? This can't be good.

"Your secret's out!" Teddy snickers. "You might as well admit it!"

The hallway starts spinning. "Are you INSANE?" I shout. "Gina's my WORST ENEMY!!"

"Not according to Artur!" crows Francis.

I feel like throwing up. You know what this means? Artur didn't get it. He was too clueless to realize I was trying to set him up with Gina.

HE THOUGHT I WANTED HER FOR **MYSELF!!**

And even worse: He BLABBED about it! Now everyone thinks I've got the hots for THE MOST OBNOXIOUS PERSON WHO EVER LIVED!! Hey, thanks a million, Artur.

The bell rings for homeroom, but I don't move. Do I really need to be in the same room with Artur and Gina right now? Maybe I'll just skip it.

But then I remember what Dad said at breakfast: that I'm not grounded anymore . . .

Skipping homeroom means detention. And detention is definitely an incident. Shoot.

I start toward Mrs. Godfrey's room.

Hickey's chasing after me, waving a piece of paper.

I recognize it right away. It's Artur's Warm Fuzzies order form. And it's PACKED.

I quickly scan it. Wow. He sold twenty on the first

day . . . fourteen the night of the "Peter Pan" show . . . then another three . . . then two . . . then five . . .

I add 'em all up.

Wait. How much? I knew Artur was selling his butt off, but THIS is RIDICULOUS. It feels like I just got punched in the stomach.

His eyes bug out. "THANKS you, Nate!" he says. "I was not even know I LOST this!" Then he lowers his voice to a whisper. "Now can you guess what nice something I did for YOU?"

He gives me a big smile and then nods like he's waiting for an answer. What does he expect me to say? I sure can't tell him the TRUTH.

"Forget about that whole thing, Artur," I say gruffly. "I like somebody else."

There. Was that simple enough for you? Maybe that'll put a stop to these ugly "Nate likes Gina" rumors.

Gina snarls at me like a rabid ferret. "I don't know what idiotic stunt you're trying to pull . . ."

I breathe a little sigh of relief. I mean, that's what I was EXPECTING her to say, but I was still sort of worried. What if THIS had happened?

There. THAT shut her up. Now I can focus on making it through the day. I just keep repeating the same two words: NO INCIDENTS!

It's exhausting. Staying out of trouble for a whole day is harder than you think. I have a close call during gym. And another in science.

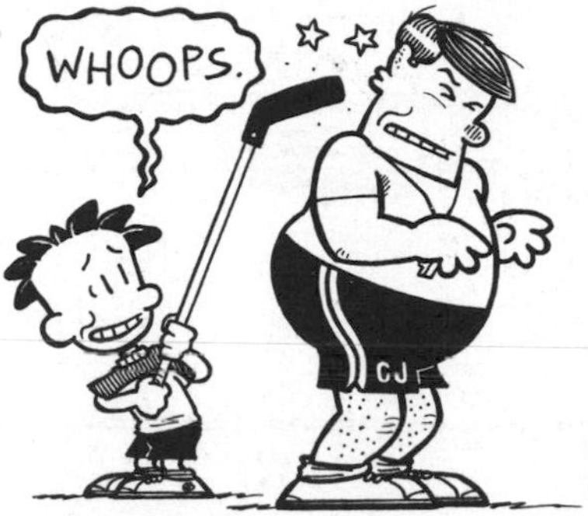
WHOOPS.
CJ

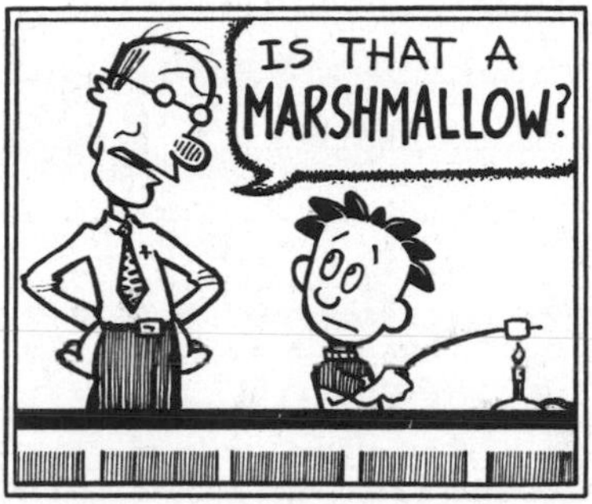
IS THAT A MARSHMALLOW?

But I make it. The bell rings. It's official: I'm not grounded anymore.

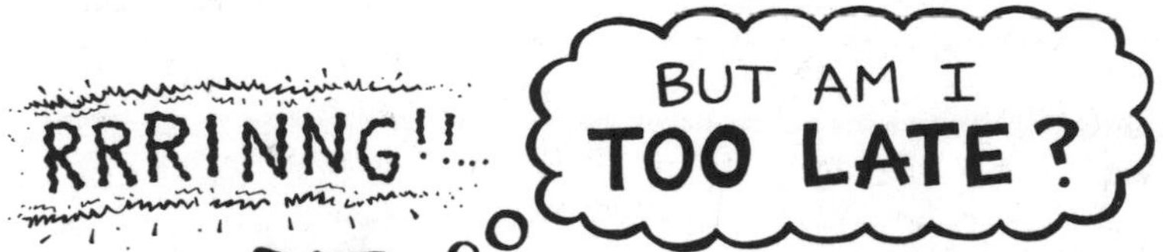
RRRINNG!!...
BUT AM I TOO LATE?

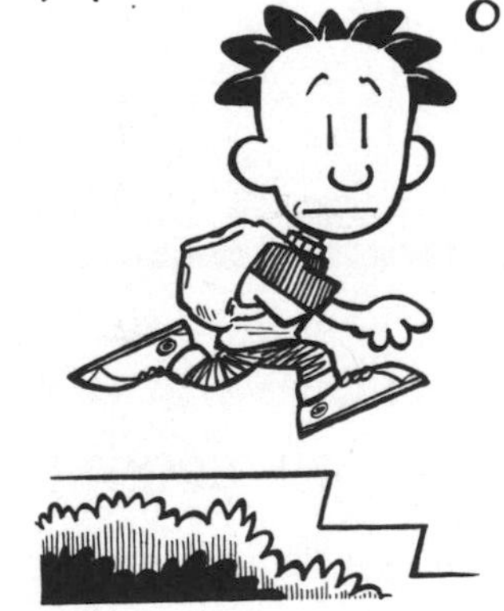

There's not much time. Our Warm Fuzzies orders are due at Thursday's troop meeting. I've got two days to catch up to Artur—if I can earn enough money.

TALLY SHEET

⊕ Wall hangings sold (5)	$	40
⊕ Walking Spitsy	$	56
⊕ Weeding garden	$	20
⊕ Moving boxes	$	15
⊕ Painting	$	12
Total earned →	$	143
minus money spent (copying)	$	33.92
GRAND TOTAL →	$	109.08

Bottom line: He's way ahead of me. To win that skateboard—and to make Artur finish SECOND for once in his stinkin' life—I've got to earn over three hundred dollars by Thursday. Impossible.

Well, no. Nothing's impossible. But it's going to be tough. I'm going to need a miracle. The question is . . .

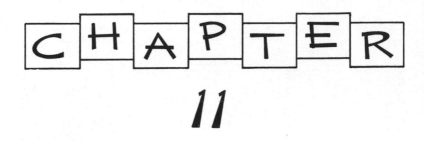

CHAPTER
11

My cheeks start to burn. "Oh . . . you heard
about that, huh?"

Gordie laughs, but not in a mean way. "Nate, you hijacked the public address system!"

Exactly. I think I'm going to skip over that scene when I write my life story. Time to change the subject. "What's that?" I ask.

"It lists the cash value of collectible comic books," he explains, handing it to me. "You wouldn't BELIEVE how much some of them are worth!"

I flip through it. Hm. I thought I knew a lot about comics, but . . .

"Sure, Nate," he says. "Bring it down to the store later."

I sprint home.

Fast.

SKATEBOARD fast.

You're probably wondering what's going on. Well, I'm not really sure. Not YET. For now, all I can tell you is this:

It might be right under my nose!

At the end of the troop meeting on Thursday, we all give our order forms to Teddy's dad.

"Guys," Artur asks us, "what is jamboree?"

"It's sort of a Timber Scout carnival," Francis says. "Every troop in the city will be there."

"It's like the Math Olympiad, Artur," I explain.

There's Artur's ride. He waves as he climbs into the car. "Well, I hope I will winning a prize!" he says. "So longs, guys!"

"He HOPES he'll win?" Teddy wonders aloud. "The way Artur's been selling those wall hangings . . ."

"Don't be so sure, boys," I say. "Artur just might have some COMPETITION!"

"I WAS." I nod.

...BUT THEN **BUMBLE BOY** CAME TO THE RESCUE!

The guys look confused. Hey, I can't say I blame them. I'd never heard of "Bumble Boy" EITHER . . . until that yard sale last fall.

nate's REAL LIFE YARD SALE COMIX!

I was on my way home from soccer practice...

Ooh! Looks like some good stuff!

YARD SALE

"So you bought some moldy old comic book," says Francis. "What does that have to do with the fund-raiser?"

"Cool your jets, Francis, there's more to the story!" I say. I tell them about Gordie and his price guide.

I couldn't believe it: A THOUSAND BUCKS!! I was almost POSITIVE I had the exact same comic book in my closet. I just wasn't sure I could FIND it.

It took a whole lot of searching. But finally . . .

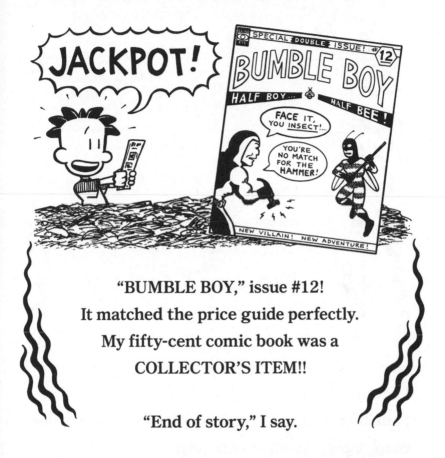

"BUMBLE BOY," issue #12!
It matched the price guide perfectly.
My fifty-cent comic book was a
COLLECTOR'S ITEM!!

"End of story," I say.

"No, Gordie's boss said it wasn't in mint condi-tion," I say. "The cover was a little bit ripped . . ."

"But he still paid me a lot. MAYBE enough to win that skateboard."

"If a skateboard was what you wanted, you could have just BOUGHT one with the 'Bumble Boy' money," Teddy points out. "You didn't have to spend it all on wall hangings."

"But then I wouldn't have raised any money for the Timber Scouts," I remind him.

"Well, how much DID you raise?" Francis asks.

"I don't want to jinx it," I say.

On Saturday morning, Francis and I walk over to the football field where the jamboree is. After we find Teddy and the rest of the guys, we walk around and check everything out.

That's when Artur starts bugging me.

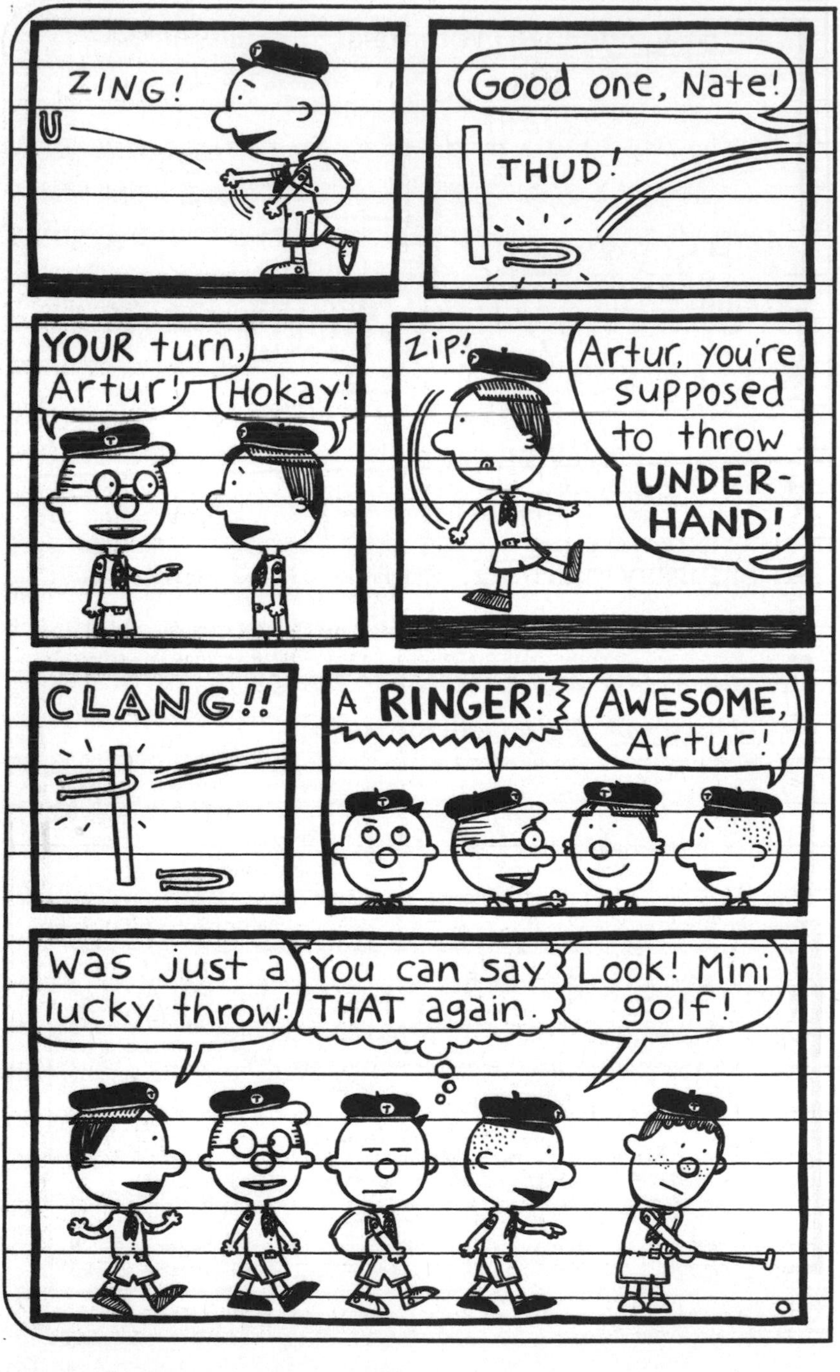

ZING!
Good one, Nate!
THUD!
YOUR turn, Artur!
Hokay!
ZIP!
Artur, you're supposed to throw UNDER-HAND!
CLANG!!
A RINGER!
AWESOME, Artur!
Was just a lucky throw!
You can say THAT again.
Look! Mini golf!

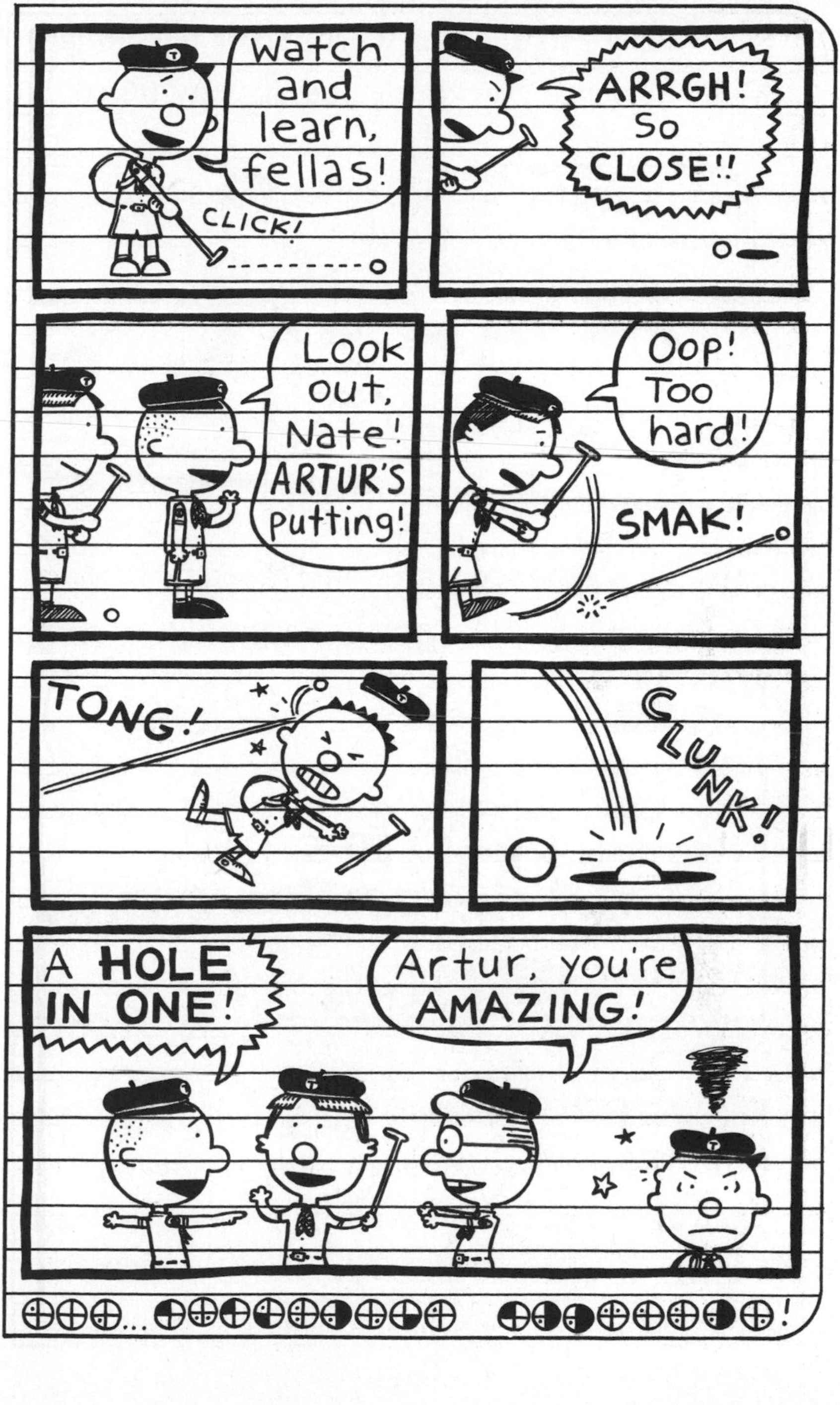
Watch and learn, fellas!
CLICK!
ARRGH! So CLOSE!!
Look out, Nate! ARTUR'S putting!
Oop! Too hard!
SMAK!
TONG!
CLUNK!
A HOLE IN ONE!
Artur, you're AMAZING!

See what it's like? Even when Artur has no idea
what he's doing, everything goes his way. It's so . . .

Oops. That's the scoutmaster. This could be it.

Yup, this is it. My stomach starts doing flip-flops.
I MIGHT have raised enough money to beat Artur.
Then again, he could have sold a lot more Warm
Fuzzies since I saw his order form on Tuesday.

And who knows? Maybe some kid from another troop sold more than BOTH of us.

"Third prize, a build-a-robot kit, goes to . . ."

...JOSH HUSKY FROM TROOP SEVEN!

Polite applause. Josh walks up front and collects his prize. I clap a few times. Or I THINK I do. I'm so nervous, I can't feel my hands.

"And now for the top two prize winners . . ." Pause.

"Artur Pashkov and Nate Wright, both of troop three! Please come on up, boys!"

Everybody's clapping. People are pushing us toward the podium. I feel numb. So that's what I get for chasing after Artur for two weeks? A TIE??

"Both these scouts sold FIFTY-EIGHT wall hangings! They EACH deserve the grand prize!" the scoutmaster announces as we reach the podium. "But there can only be ONE WINNER!"

What? Really? THAT'S how we're deciding who gets the skateboard? A coin flip between me . . .

Technically, I know I've got a fifty-fifty chance.

But it doesn't feel that way. Not against Mr. Lucky. It feels more like a one out of ten chance. Or one out of a HUNDRED.

The scoutmaster nods my way. "Call it, young man." And before I can even think about it, the coin's in the air.

"Heads it is!"

Heads? So . . . I win?

"And Nate . . ." the scoutmaster says.

" . . . along with a certificate to have it custom painted at Ben's Board & Wheel!"

"Thanks," I manage to say, holding tight to the skateboard. MY skateboard. I can't stop staring at it. I guess Artur DOESN'T always win!

Suddenly he's right beside me. He holds out his hand. "Good jobs, Nate," he says.

YOU ARE **DESERVE** GRAND PRIZE!

I can't tell if he means it or not. See why Artur's so tough to figure out? He just lost something he tried really hard to win . . . but he still acts HAPPY for me. It's weird.

"I am invite all the guys to my house to set up my telescope!" he says.

COME ON!

"You go ahead, Artur," I tell him.

Lincoln Peirce

BiG NATE

GOES FOR BROKE

For Beanie and Poppa

CHAPTER 1

I don't want to brag or anything, but I happen to be the president of the greatest club ever invented.

Our official name is the P.S. 38 Cartooning Club, but we call ourselves the Doodlers. We meet every Wednesday after school in the art studio, and we sit around drawing comics until the custodian kicks us out. It's the best club in the whole school. By a MILE. Don't believe me? Well, then, check out this lineup.

PROBLEM SOLVERS – a bunch of eggheads hanging out in the computer lab doing ridiculously hard math problems… **FOR FUN!!**

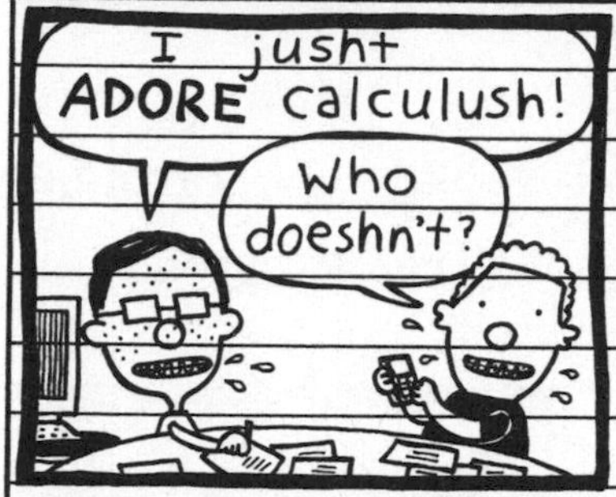

I jusht ADORE calculush!
Who doeshn't?

WHY IT'S LAME: Isn't it obvious?

SPOTLIGHT CLUB – for kids who are convinced they're going to be huge recording stars

WHY IT'S LAME:

A. They're constantly singing in public in the hopes of being "discovered."

B. They can't sing.

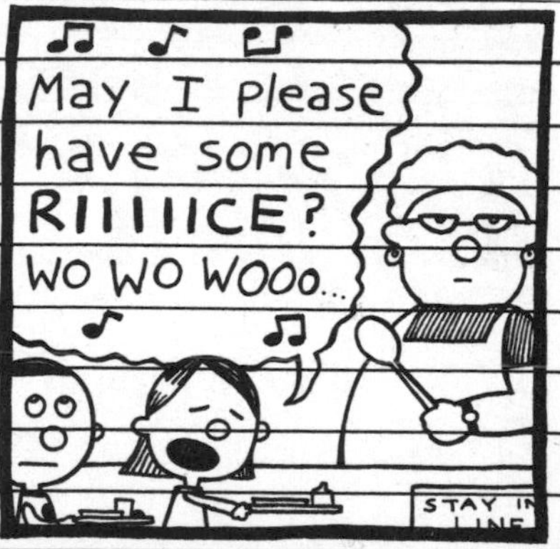

May I please have some RIIIIICE? WO WO WOOo…
STAY IN

SCHOOL BEAUTIFICATION SOCIETY – just what it sounds like

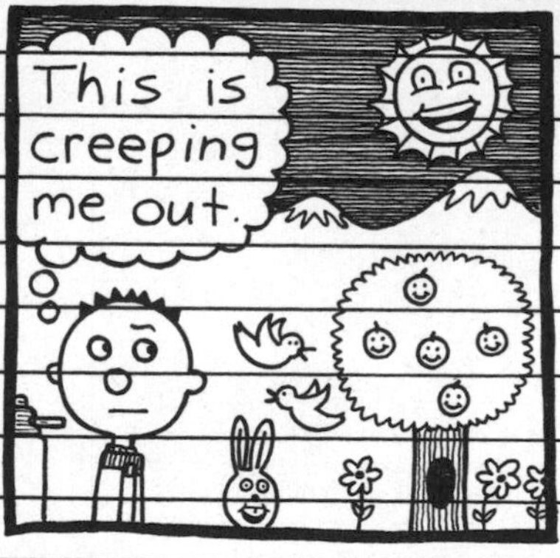

This is creeping me out.

WHY IT'S LAME: Apparently, "beautification" means painting cheesy murals in the second-floor boys' bathroom.

See? Most of these so-called clubs look about as fun as an ingrown toenail.

But the Doodlers rock. And we only got started a few months ago. That's when it all came together . . .

...THANKS TO A GLOB OF PEANUT BUTTER!

DRAMATIC FLASHBACK

It was a typical social studies class.

Mrs. Godfrey was babbling about some dead guy who wasn't a good enough president to get his picture on any money . . .

YAK YAK YAK YAK YAK YAK YAK YAK YAK YAK YAK
blah blah Franklin Pierce blah blah
blah blah Franklin Pierce

Gina had already asked about nineteen completely useless questions in a row . . .

. . . and I was about five seconds away from falling into a coma.

Then Glenn Swenson walked by my desk on his way to the pencil sharpener . . .

. . . and suddenly things got a LOT more interesting!

He had food on his face. That's nothing new. Glenn usually has enough crumbs stuck on him to feed a family of four. But this was different. He had a glob of peanut butter the size of a hubcap . . .

He had no clue it was there. And neither did anybody else. It was hilarious. But I couldn't just crack up in the middle of class. Not unless I wanted She-Who-Must-Not-Be-Named to go Full Godfrey on me. So I did what I always do when something funny happens:

I drew a cartoon about it!

It was a good cartoon. Too good to keep to myself.

Teachers always ask that. What was I supposed to say . . . YES? Then even Glenn, who's dumber than a bag of hammers, would have realized I was making fun of him. And that would have been a problem, because whenever Glenn gets mad at people, he chases them down during recess and crushes them into the school yard fence until they can't breathe.

I decided I wanted to keep breathing.

Things went downhill from there. Mrs. Godfrey took my drawing and stuck it in her desk. Then she gave me a little pink slip of paper.

Hello, detention. And hello, Mrs. Czerwicki.

What could I say? She was right. But she didn't stop there. Mrs. Czerwicki didn't realize it, but the next thing out of her mouth was about to CHANGE THE COURSE OF CARTOONING HISTORY!!!

I have to admit, it was a brilliant idea—even for me. I ran and asked Principal Nichols if I could start a cartooning club . . .

Oop! It's almost 3:00. The bell's going to ring in 5 . . . 4 . . . 3 . . . 2 . . . 1 . . .

We all make a pit stop at our lockers, then head for the art studio. The art teacher, Mr. Rosa, is our faculty adviser.

Every club has an adviser. That's school policy. But most clubs have one already in place. Ms. Clarke has always run the school newspaper. And Mr. Galvin has been the adviser for the Science Club since the last Ice Age.

That's okay if you end up liking your adviser. But what if you join some club, and the adviser's horrible? Then you're just like that glob of peanut butter on Glenn Swenson's forehead. You're stuck.

That's where the Doodlers got lucky. Since we started our club from scratch, WE got to decide who our adviser would be. I mean, can you imagine if we'd ended up with somebody like . . .

Everybody freezes. We're all thinking the same thing: What's HE doing here? Did the school switch advisers on us or something? My stomach starts churning as I picture a Doodlers meeting with Coach John in charge.

Finally Francis speaks up. "Uh . . . where's Mr. Rosa?" he asks nervously.

Coach John chuckles in sort of a scary way. Did I mention the guy's a few peas short of a casserole?

"And here I am!" comes a voice from behind us.

"Sorry I'm a bit late, everyone," he says as he takes off his jacket. Then he pats Coach John on the shoulder. "Thanks for covering for me, Coach."

Coach John grunts something in return, then waddles out of the room. Finally we can all exhale.

"Listen, gang, before we get started, there's someone I'd like you to meet," Mr. Rosa tells us as we sit down. He motions toward the door.

Colleague? What's THAT supposed to mean? This lady doesn't work at P.S. 38.

"Hi, Doodlers." She smiles as she pulls a folder from her tote bag. "I'm delighted Mr. Rosa invited me to visit with you today."

Chad raises his hand. "Are YOU a cartoonist?"

She laughs. "I'm a teacher who TRIES to be a cartoonist. But that's not why I'm here."

Whoa, WHAT? Did she say "another cartooning club"?

"We call it the C.I.C., the Cartooning & Illustration Club," she continues. "We've got about thirty boys and girls at our weekly meetings."

Uh . . . girls? I feel my face getting warm. The guys sort of steal looks at each other, but nobody says anything.

"You know," she says cheerfully, "there are plenty of girls who enjoy cartooning!" Then she spreads a whole bunch of drawings around the table.

My jaw just about hits the floor as I look down at them. Same with the rest of the guys. Even Artur's eyes are as big as pie plates. He can really draw, but some of these make his stuff look like stick figures. These drawings are PRO.

"Who—who did these?" Teddy stammers.

"Why, the C.I.C., of course," Mrs. Everett answers. "My students!"

There's a stunned silence.

"WHAT students?" Chad finally asks.

I swallow hard. I think I already know the answer. But when she says it out loud, it still hits me like a brick in the head.

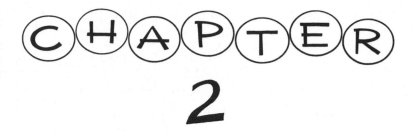

CHAPTER 2

Of course. Of all the schools to have a bigger and better cartooning club than the Doodlers . . .

Jefferson Middle School and P.S. 38 are archrivals. That's how WE feel about it, anyway. But the kids from Jefferson don't exactly see it like that.

And you know what stinks? They're RIGHT.

Jefferson always beats us. ALWAYS. In the whole time I've been at P.S. 38, we haven't won ANYTHING against them.

Their athletes are more athletic . . .

Their musicians are more musical . . .

Even their math geeks are geekier.

Sure, I know that winning isn't everything. How could I NOT? The teachers and coaches remind us a zillion times a day.

Have FUN? Hey, that's fine when you're six years old, playing T-ball for Little Ducklings Day Care. But after a while, that whole let's-give-everyone-a-trophy thing gets pretty tired. We're not babies anymore. We want to WIN.

"I wonder how long it's been since P.S. 38 actually beat Jefferson," Teddy says.

"What a coincidence you should mention that!" Francis chimes in. "Just for kicks, I was browsing through the school archives . . ."

"SEVEN YEARS? What'd we win at?" Teddy asks.

"Debating, I think," Francis answers.

". . . next Saturday!"

Teddy's right. I've been trying not to think about it too much—I don't want to jinx us—but our basketball team plays Jefferson next week for the first time since last year's conference championship.

What a fiasco THAT was. But this year's going to be different. We're better than we were last season, for one thing. And it's a home game for us.

A snowball slams into my head. Everything goes dark for a second, and then I land face-first in a puddle of slush. Chunks of snow are starting to slide down the back of my shirt. I jump up.

At first I can't tell who they are; they're scrunched down behind a stone wall at the top of a little hill.

But then one of them stands, and I see it: a purple jacket with gold sleeves and a big gold *J* on the chest.

We start up the hill, but it's no use. They've got a huge pile of pre-made snowballs. For every handful of snow we scoop up and throw at them, they send a dozen back at us. It's like an avalanche. There's only one thing to do:

We run for half a block until we're out of range . . .
of the snowballs, that is. But we can still hear them
laughing at us . . .

. . . LOUD AND CLEAR!

"That was Nolan," Teddy says,
breathing hard.

"Who?"

"He lives near me," Teddy says matter-of-factly.
"He's kind of a jerk."

"Oh, really?" I snap, trying to shake the snow out of my pants.

I should probably explain something. Maybe you only have one middle school in your town. But in OUR town, there are FIVE of 'em. And Jefferson's close to P.S. 38. It's practically in the same neighborhood. That's why the rivalry is such a big deal: because we KNOW a lot of those kids.

"Can we talk about something besides Jefferson?" Francis says.

"Okay," he continues. "What did you guys think of what Mrs. Everett said at the Doodlers meeting?"

"I meant what she said about the club not having any girls."

I shrug. The only answer I can come up with sounds pretty lame:

"Girls can join if they WANT to," Teddy says. "It's just that none of them have asked."

"We haven't asked THEM, either," Francis says, sounding more and more like my dad. "Maybe we should."

Francis gets all exasperated. "That's the whole POINT, you pinhead!"

I know what Teddy's getting at. Yeah, there are some girls who'd probably make good Doodlers . . .

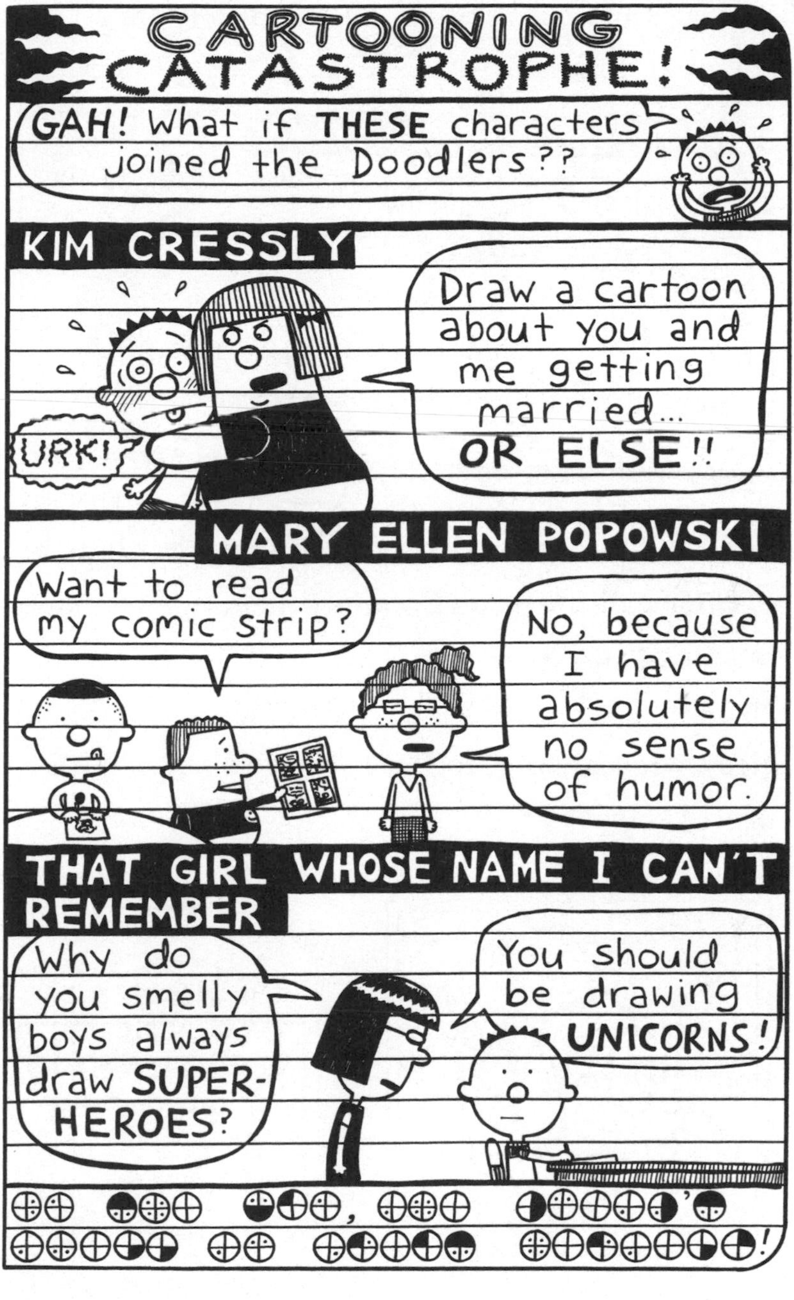

CARTOONING CATASTROPHE!
GAH! What if THESE characters joined the Doodlers??
KIM CRESSLY
URK!
Draw a cartoon about you and me getting married... OR ELSE!!
MARY ELLEN POPOWSKI
Want to read my comic strip?
No, because I have absolutely no sense of humor.
THAT GIRL WHOSE NAME I CAN'T REMEMBER
Why do you smelly boys always draw SUPER-HEROES?
You should be drawing UNICORNS!

I shiver, but not because of the snow. The thought of Gina walking into a Doodlers meeting just made my blood run cold.

"Hey, what about Dee Dee?" Francis says. "SHE'S pretty artsy!"

SHE DESIGNS ALL THE POSTERS FOR THE SCHOOL PLAYS!

"She's such a DRAMA QUEEN, though." Teddy frowns.

"Speaking of Dee Dee," I say, "that sounded sort of like her."

"It IS her," Teddy says as she comes closer. "Acting like she's onstage, as usual."

Francis shakes his head. "I don't think she's acting," he says seriously. All three of us run to meet her.

"Dee Dee! What's wrong?" Francis says.

CHAPTER 3

When we reach Chad, he's lying on his back in the middle of the sidewalk like a flipped-over turtle.

Take it easy, Dee Dee. You're not a doctor. And playing Nurse Ouchie in our second grade production of "Bunny Gets a Boo-Boo" doesn't mean you know what you're talking about.

"Where does it hurt, Chad?" Francis asks.

"My butt," Chad groans.

With a flourish, Dee Dee pulls out her cell phone.

"An emergency?" Teddy repeats. "It's a sore butt!"

"I wouldn't be so sure," Francis says as we help Chad to his feet. "I have a different diagnosis."

"How TRAGIC!" Dee Dee wails, as if we'd just told Chad he has two weeks to live.

See why Teddy called her a drama queen? She can take any situation and turn it into a major theatrical production. Starring herself.

We ignore her. "Can you walk?" I ask Chad.

He takes a couple steps, then winces. "I CAN," he says miserably. "But it doesn't feel very good."

So Dee Dee calls Chad's mom, and we wait with him until she shows up.

"Alas," says Dee Dee as they drive off. "Poor Chad."

Poor Chad is right. The next day in school, he's sitting on a donut.

A MEDICAL donut, I mean. It's a giant inflatable ring, almost like a life preserver. When he walks from class to class, it looks like he's carrying a toilet seat.

So Francis was right. It WAS his tailbone.

I feel bad for Chad. Not just because he's hurt, but because . . . well, having a bruised tailbone is sort of embarrassing, don't you think? I mean, when you're talking about different kinds of injuries . . .

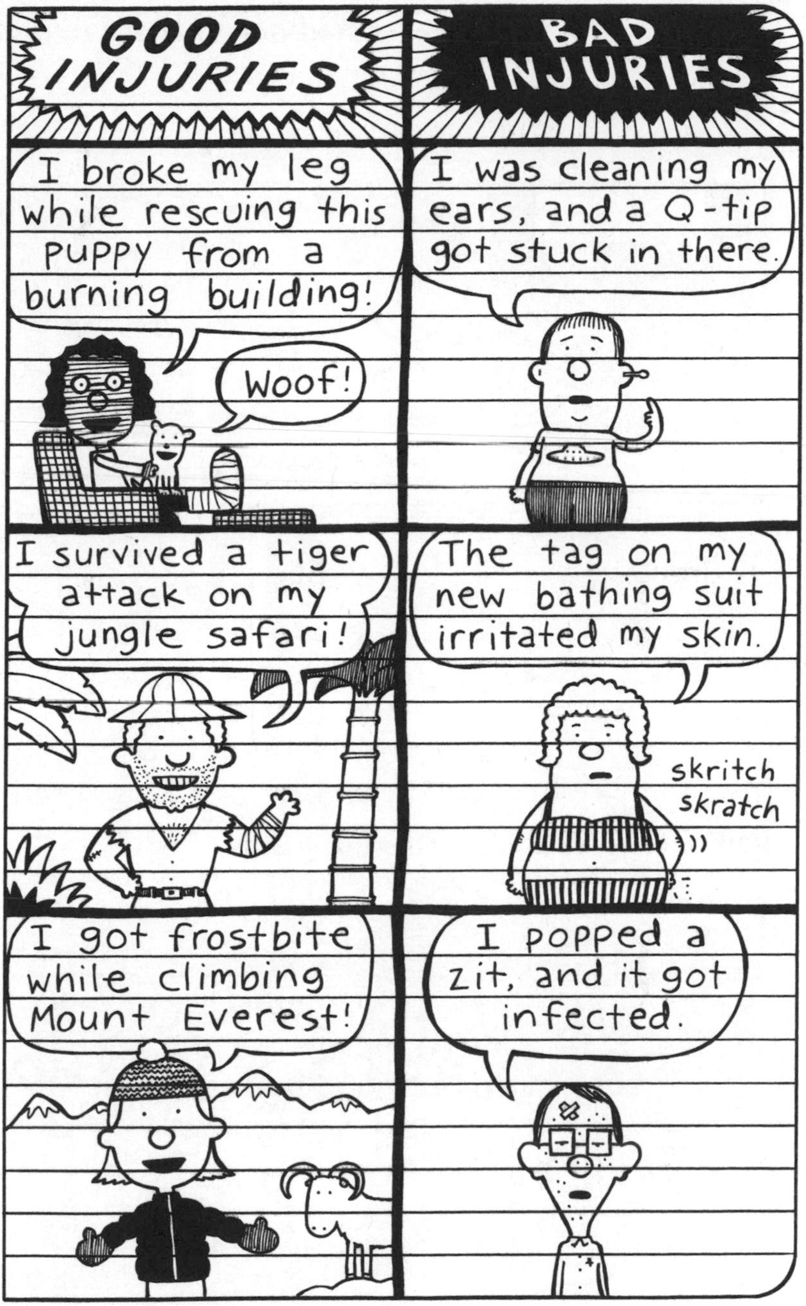
GOOD INJURIES
BAD INJURIES
I broke my leg while rescuing this puppy from a burning building!
Woof!
I was cleaning my ears, and a Q-tip got stuck in there.
I survived a tiger attack on my jungle safari!
The tag on my new bathing suit irritated my skin.
skritch skratch
I got frostbite while climbing Mount Everest!
I popped a zit, and it got infected.

I've been lucky. I've never had one of those really embarrassing injuries.

"Good gravy!" Mr. Rosa yelps in surprise. "Nate, are you all right?"

"Yeah. I'm okay," I say as I get off the floor.

"Well, since you're all here," Mr. Rosa continues, "I'd like to mention that Mrs. Everett made a good point yesterday . . ."

Not THIS again. Why do we have to change the club? Why mess with perfection?

"Boys aren't the ONLY ones who wind up in detention for drawing comics." Mr. Rosa chuckles. "Girls can be pretty cartoony, too!"

We watch as he disappears down the hallway. "Recruiting," I grumble. "Whoop-de-stinkin'-do."

"Who are we supposed to recruit?" Teddy wonders.

Uh, right WHERE? All I see is a poster for the dance tomorrow night.

"DEE DEE drew that!" Francis explains.

I examine the poster. Okay, three cheers for Dee Dee. She can draw a half-decent seagull. But why does that mean she gets to join the Doodlers? I don't want our meetings

turning into the Amazing Dee Dee Show.

"Aren't there any other girls we can recruit?" I ask hopefully.

Teddy jumps in. "What about Jenny?"

I cringe. Jenny would be an AWESOME Doodler. That's obvious. But there's one huge problem:

And—don't ask me why—Jenny and Artur are still an item. So if she joined the club, Wednesday afternoons would probably turn into . . .

Ugh. I'm supposed to draw comics while those two count each other's freckles? I'd rather eat egg salad. Hey, I'd rather BATHE in egg salad.

"I already talked to Jenny," I lie. "She can't do it."

"Then it's decided!" Francis declares with a clap of his hands. "Dee Dee it is!"

Teddy grimaces. "Who's going to ask her?"

"We'll shoot for it," Teddy says. "Odds or evens?"

"Evens," I say automatically. I ALWAYS pick evens.

ONCE...
TWICE...
THREE TIMES...

...SHOOT!

ODDS! I WIN!

CONGRATULATIONS, NATE! THE JOB'S ALL **YOURS**!

Rats. I KNEW I should have picked odds.

I walk into the cafetorium, racking my brain for a way to weasel out of this. Then I remember the last thing Mr. Rosa told us:

And talk about timing. Guess who's sitting at the very first table? Dee Dee and her flock of BFFs from the Drama Club.

She doesn't hear me. Why am I not surprised?

"DEE DEE!" I yell a few dozen times. Finally she turns around.

"What is it, Nate?" Dee Dee says.

"Hm? Uh . . . well, it's . . ." I stammer. "I . . . um . . . wanted to ask you something."

"Okay, go ahead!"

A half-eaten sandwich flies past us, nearly clocking me in the head. For a second, I lose my train of thought.

"I . . . uh . . . I forgot what I was saying," I tell her, a little flustered.

"It's okay," Dee Dee chirps. "I know what you were about to ask, and SURE! . . ."

CHAPTER 4

Okay, let's get something straight: I'd ask MRS. GODFREY to the dance before I'd ask Dee Dee. But I guess that doesn't matter now.

What matters is, she THOUGHT I was asking her. Before I could explain, she'd already turned lunchtime into show-and-tell.

Dee Dee has a voice that could blow a hole in a battleship, so right then and there the whole cafetorium knew: She and I were going to the dance together.

That's how I ended up here: half a block from her

house at 7:10 on Friday night.

For a second, I think about going home. But that would never work. The Parent Patrol would see to that.

Besides, I don't want to miss the dance. They're cheesy, but I LIKE school dances. And I actually know what I'm doing out there—unlike SOME people. Check out these so-called moves:

P.S. 38 DANCE FLOOR of SHAME!

STARRING...

FRANCIS

He's my best friend, but what a stiff. He moves like a 3-toed sloth in a full body cast.

THE CHEERLEADING SQUAD

They dance together in a big group, and whenever a good song starts, they all go completely berserk.

SETH QUINCY aka "Q-TIP"

Picture a scarecrow in a wind tunnel. When Q-Tip starts flailing around, his elbows and knees turn into lethal weapons.

Anyway, it looks like I'm stuck taking Dee Dee to the dance. But how do I do it . . .

Answer: I have absolutely no idea. But I definitely don't want everybody thinking I'm Dee Dee's soul mate. I've got to tell her right now . . .

Yikes. Where did Dee Dee shampoo her hair—in the produce section at Grocery Town? I'm so surprised by the pyramid of fruit on her head that I forget about my "just friends" speech. I guess I'll tell her while we walk to the dance.

Or maybe not. I try, but I can't get a word in edgewise. Dee Dee never stops yakking. I don't get it: When does she come up for air?

By the time we reach the school, I've heard enough of the World According to Dee Dee to last awhile. Like forever. We step into the lobby and . . .

Ugh. It's Randy Betancourt, P.S. 38's resident scuzzball. He's just like Chad's tailbone: a total pain in the butt.

He snickers and shoots us one of his typical Randy smirks. Briefly, I consider hitting him in his big fat nose with a piece of fruit. After all, Dee Dee's got a head full of ammo. Then . . .

The smirk slides off Randy's face in half a heartbeat. He looks totally stunned. Hey, I'm a little stunned myself. Did that just really HAPPEN?

She shrugs. "He deserved it," she says as we hang up our coats. "If two friends want to go to a dance together . . ."

I could remind Dee Dee that SHE can make a big deal out of sharpening a pencil, but I decide not to. I'm too busy breathing a huge sigh of relief. Did you hear what she just called us?

So she DOESN'T like me! Not in "THAT" sort of way. I can relax. Dee Dee's not going to turn all sappy and start calling me stupid pet names like Lamb Chop, Dumpling Face, Puffy Bunny, Snuggle Bug . . .

...HONEYBEE, SUGAR BOOGER, PASSION PANDA...

NATE!... HELLOooo? NATE!

I'M GOING TO CHANGE INTO MY BEACH CLOTHES.

Good idea. I grab my backpack and slip into the bathroom. I'm still feeling pretty pumped. Knowing Dee Dee isn't

BOYS

all gung ho to make me her love monkey has flipped this whole evening completely around.

He disappears, and all my clothes go with him. I look down at what I'm wearing, and a sick feeling settles in my gut. Tighty-whities and a pair of tube socks won't cut it as "beach attire."

I peek out, hoping I'll spot a friendly face. And hoping nobody spots ME. It would be just my luck to run into a reporter from the school newspaper right about now.

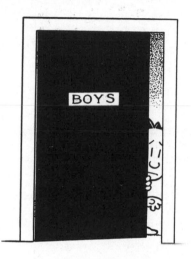

The lobby's empty. Everybody's gone into the gym. Unless I want to stroll in there looking like an escapee from a nudist colony, I'm stuck.

She stops, then inches slowly toward me. "Nate?" she asks. "What are you doing?"

I hesitate. This is pretty embarrassing. But what do I have to lose? We're FRIENDS, right? Dee Dee said so herself. And I need help.

She scowls. "He's an even bigger moron than I THOUGHT he was," she grumbles. Then her face brightens.

Wait right here? That's hilarious. Where does she think I'd go?

This must be some Drama Queen Rule: Always be ready for a costume change. I don't know what's in that bag, but I'm not picky. It's got to be better than what I'M wearing.

"You look fabulous!" Dee Dee beams.

"FABULOUS?" I shout in disbelief. "I'm wearing a DRESS!"

"It's a grass skirt, genius," she says matter-of-factly as she drags me toward the gym.

Great. Hawaii is five thousand miles away, and I look like an idiot. But why sweat the details?

Into the gym we go, with me praying that everyone's too busy dancing to notice me. But then . . .

A bunch of kids gather around. I brace myself.

Wait, what's going on here? No finger pointing? No insults? What's WRONG with these people?

"That's AMAZING, Nate!" someone says. "You look just LIKE them!"

I'm about to ask who "them" is . . . and then I look up at the stage.

I'm dressed exactly like the band. Or they're dressed exactly like me.

"You must KNOW those guys, right?" one kid says.

"How'd you pull it off, Nate?" asks another.

"It . . . well . . . uh . . ." I stammer. I can't think of a single word to say. But Dee Dee can.

And that's that. I get a few more compliments, and then everybody starts dancing again, leaving me and Dee Dee standing by the snack table.

Hmmm. NOW what? I should probably say something to her, like:

That's not what comes out, though. Instead, it's:

"From the Drama Club," she says. Then she strikes a pose and gives a sigh so huge, it practically blows my shirt off. "I just love the Drama Club."

Yes, Dee Dee, we know. Without the Drama Club, life would have no meaning.

Suddenly I remember what I was doing when this whole thing started: RECRUITING!

I tell her about the club and what an awesome adviser Mr. Rosa is. I talk about the fun drawing games we play at meetings, like Add-On, Connect-the-Freckles, and Going, Going, Godfrey.

"AND," I add, "if you join, you'll be the first girl Doodler EVER."

"I'm in," she announces immediately.

"Excellent!" I say, and I mean it, too. Sort of.

"Let's boogie!" Dee Dee shouts, and she and I hit the dance floor.

Whew. Except for the fact that my clothes are probably stuffed in a garbage can somewhere, this all turned out pretty well! I still

think Dee Dee needs to hit the off button on the drama-tron, but she kept this dance from becoming a total disaster. She's okay.

"Do you feel something wet?" she asks suddenly.

Huh? WET? That's weird. Maybe one of those tangerines on her head just sprang a leak.

CHAPTER 5

THE AMAZING ADVENTURES OF
ULTRA-NATE
SUPER 6TH GRADER!
TODAY'S EPISODE: "RAIN DANCE"
costarring DEE DEE
TA-DAH!
HEY!

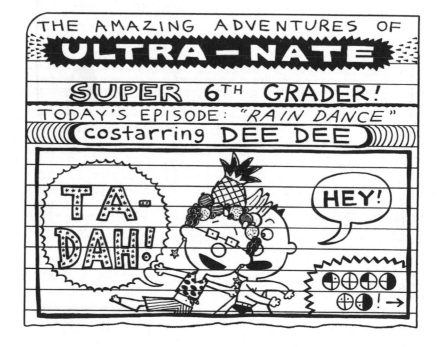

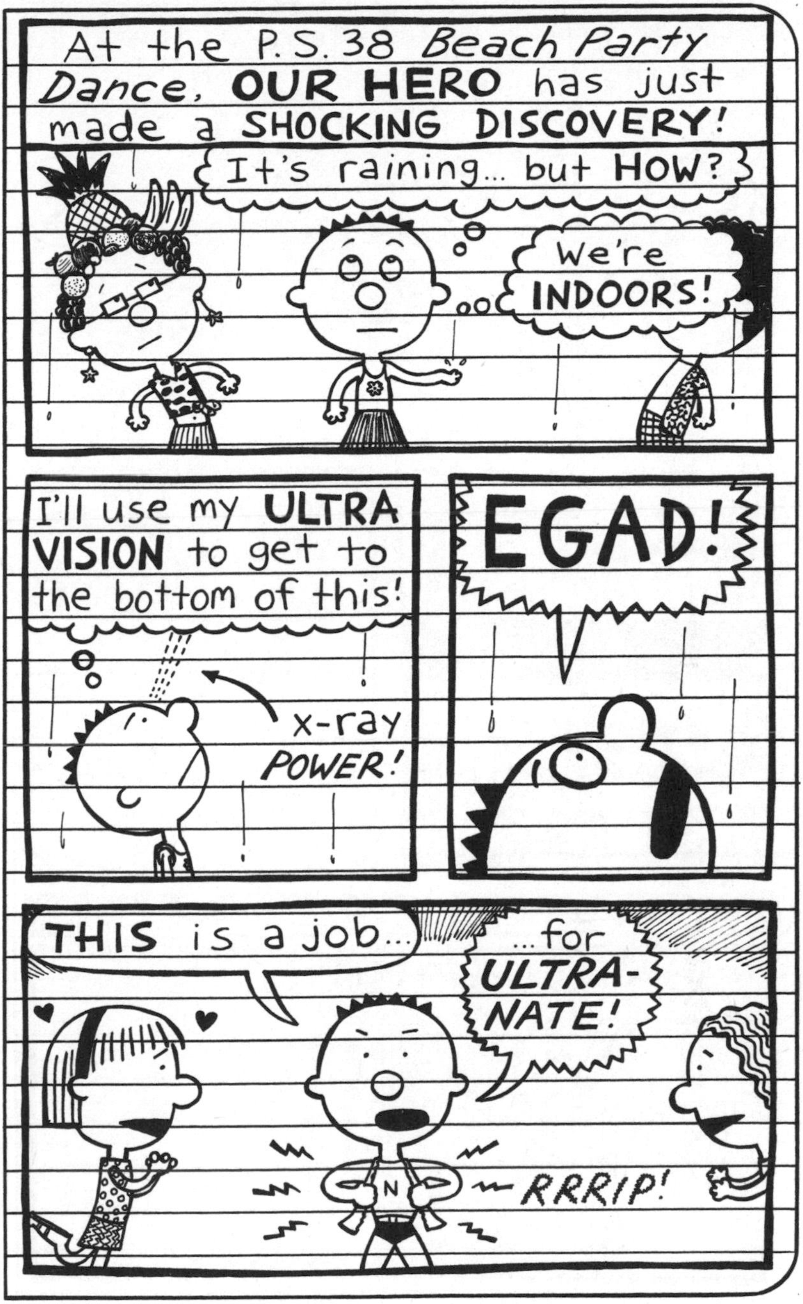
At the P.S. 38 *Beach Party Dance*, **OUR HERO** has just made a **SHOCKING DISCOVERY!**
It's raining... but **HOW?**
We're **INDOORS!**
I'll use my **ULTRA VISION** to get to the bottom of this!
x-ray *POWER!*
EGAD!
THIS is a job...
...for **ULTRA-NATE!**
N
RRRIP!

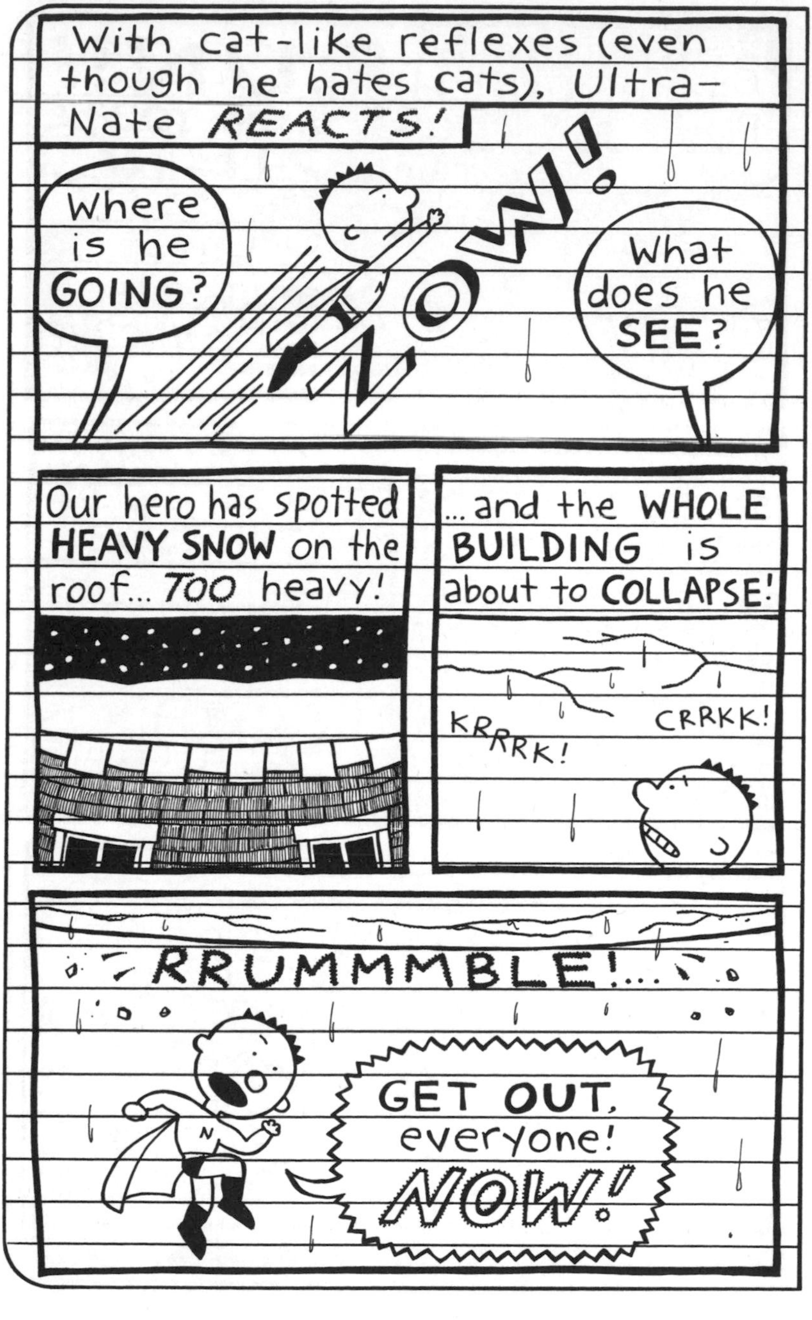

With cat-like reflexes (even though he hates cats), Ultra-Nate REACTS!
Where is he GOING?
ZOOM!
What does he SEE?
Our hero has spotted HEAVY SNOW on the roof... TOO heavy!
...and the WHOLE BUILDING is about to COLLAPSE!
KRRRRK!
CRRKK!
RRUMMMBLE!...
GET OUT, everyone! NOW!

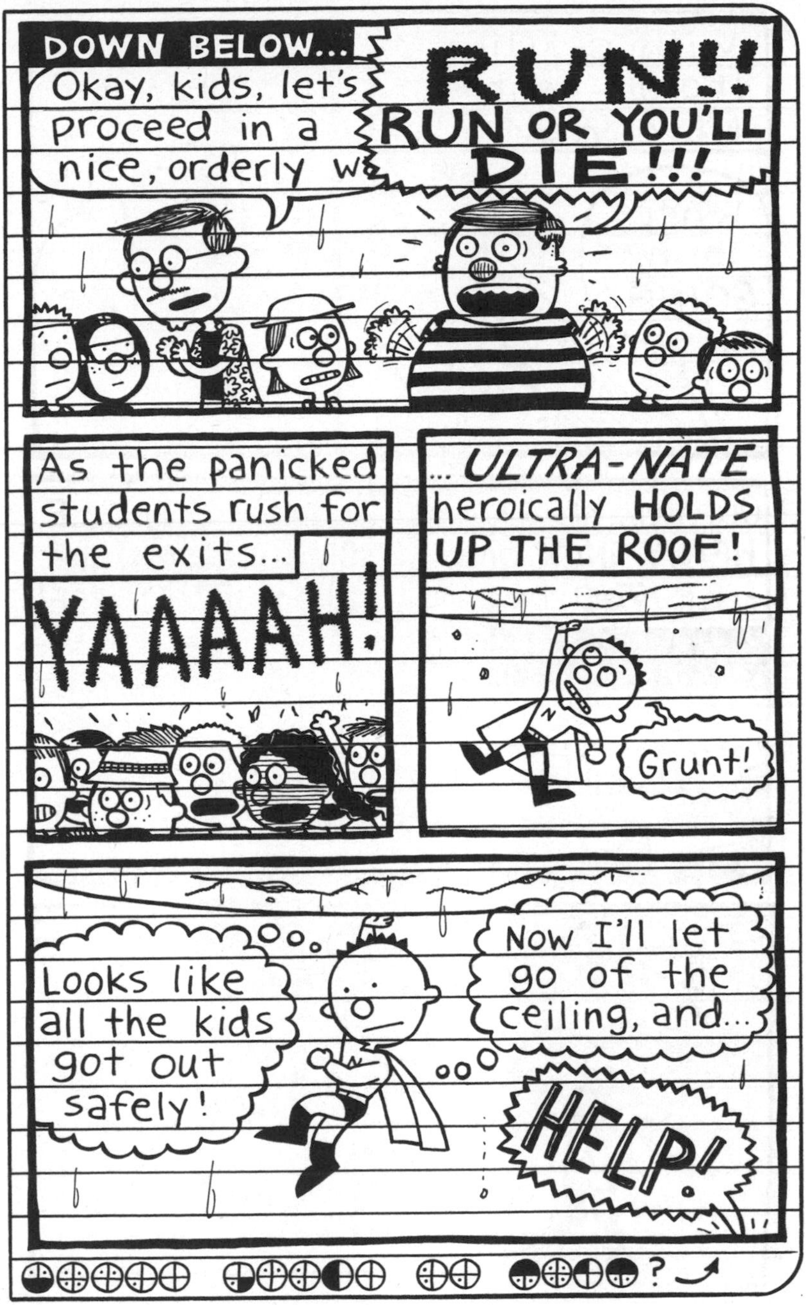

DOWN BELOW...
Okay, kids, let's proceed in a nice, orderly w
RUN!! RUN OR YOU'LL DIE!!!
As the panicked students rush for the exits...
YAAAAH!
...ULTRA-NATE heroically HOLDS UP THE ROOF!
Grunt!
Looks like all the kids got out safely!
Now I'll let go of the ceiling, and...
HELP!

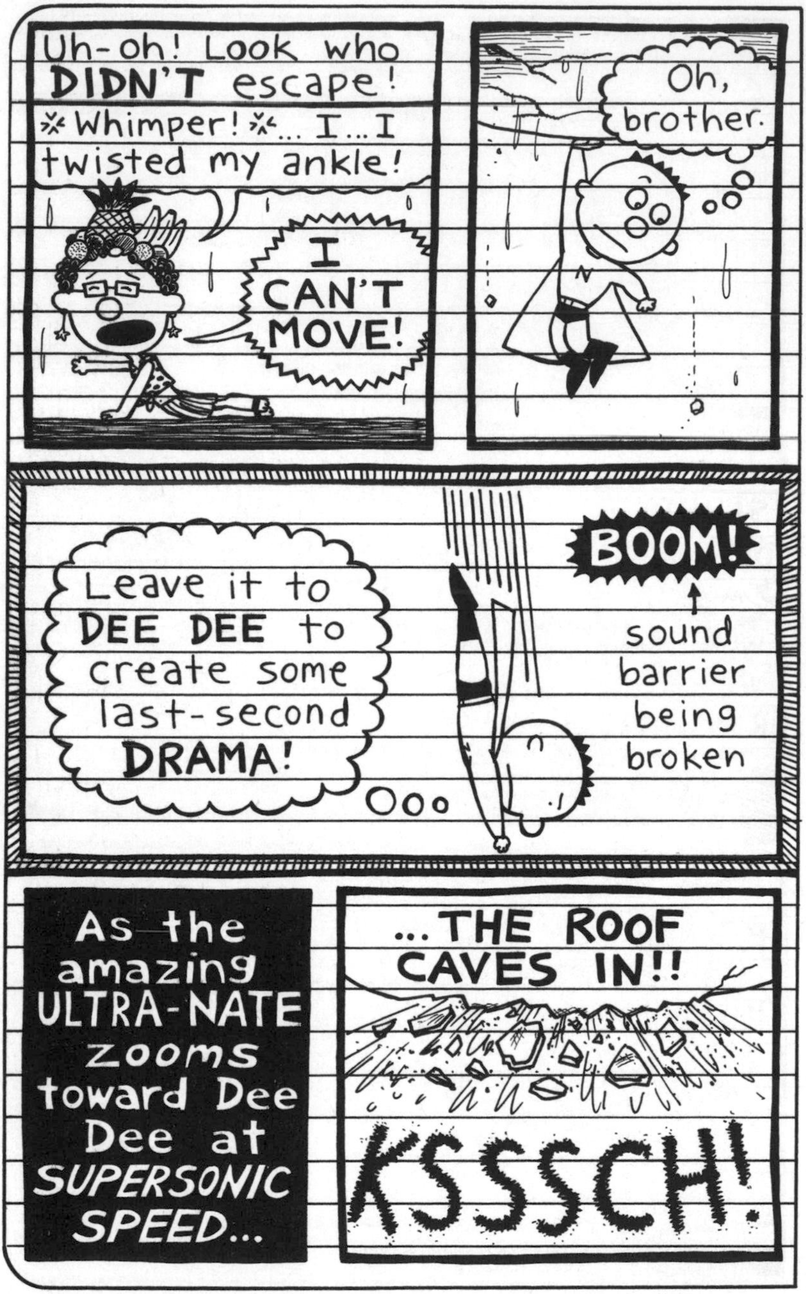
Uh-oh! Look who DIDN'T escape!
Whimper! ... I ... I twisted my ankle!
I CAN'T MOVE!
Oh, brother.
Leave it to DEE DEE to create some last-second DRAMA!
BOOM!
sound barrier being broken
As the amazing ULTRA-NATE zooms toward Dee Dee at SUPERSONIC SPEED...
... THE ROOF CAVES IN!!
KSSSCH!

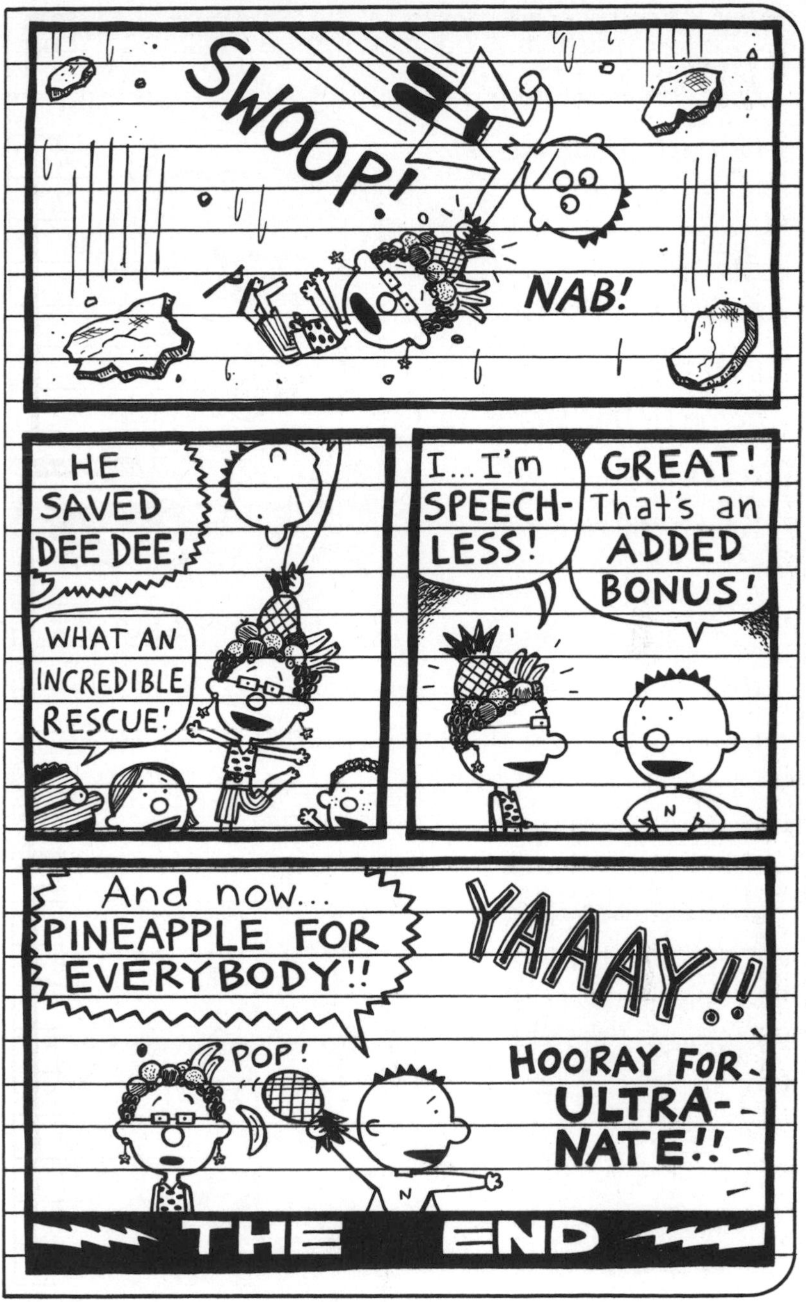
SWOOP!
NAB!
HE SAVED DEE DEE!
WHAT AN INCREDIBLE RESCUE!
I... I'm SPEECH-LESS!
GREAT! That's an ADDED BONUS!
And now... PINEAPPLE FOR EVERYBODY!!
YAAAY!!
POP!
HOORAY FOR ULTRA-NATE!!
THE END

Okay, it might not have happened EXACTLY like that. I was using a little something we cartoonists call artistic license.

But it DID start raining inside the gym. And I DID come to Dee Dee's rescue . . . sort of. Here's the real story:

The chaperones didn't even NOTICE the rain at first. They were too busy stuffing their faces at the snack table. But then the fire alarm went off. THAT made them step away from the bean dip.

But there wasn't a fire. And the rain wasn't coming from a leaky roof, either. After they'd hustled us out of the gym and into the lobby, Principal Nichols explained what was going on.

Dee Dee looked crushed. "Well, THAT isn't very dramatic," she grumbled.

"I'm afraid we'll have to end the dance a little early," Principal Nichols went on.

THEN things got crazy. We were all looking for our stuff in a giant mosh pit, it was still raining, the fire alarm was still ringing, and Coach John was marching around like a deranged drill sergeant.

Once I stepped outside, it was like walking into a giant snow globe. Don't get me wrong— I love snow. But ever wear a grass skirt in a blizzard? My butt felt like a frozen Popsicle.

Mmm, marshmallows! My favorite food group. I started to follow the guys, but then . . .

"Uh . . . maybe they'll show up in the lost and found on Monday," I told her. Translation: Life happens, Dee Dee. Deal with it.

"But what about NOW?" she wailed. "I can't walk home in the snow wearing SANDALS!"

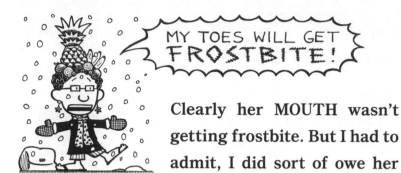

Clearly her MOUTH wasn't getting frostbite. But I had to admit, I did sort of owe her one. If it wasn't for Dee Dee . . .

Talk about a lousy end to a lousy night. Not only did I carry Dee Dee home on my back, I had to listen to her reenact scenes from her favorite horse movies.

Note to self: NEVER, not even by accident, invite a girl to a dance again.

I see a blinking light flash from Francis's window. That's our secret signal! I grab my binoculars and peer through the snow across the yard.

Tomorrow can't get here fast enough!

At exactly 10:00 the next morning, Francis and I are standing at the base of Cluffy's cliff. It's not really  a cliff, I guess. But it's the steepest hill in town. It's perfect for sledding.

"I wonder where Teddy is," I say.

Francis's eyes widen as he looks behind me. "Wow!" he shouts. "TEDDY!"

A **SUPA-SNO TUBE!** DUDE! WHERE'D YOU **GET** THAT?

"Bought it myself!" Teddy answers proudly. "I saved the money I made shoveling driveways!"

Now I'm REALLY stoked about taking on Cluffy's cliff. We hike up to the top and, after going on a couple runs himself, Teddy lets Francis and me have a turn. It's amazing.

"That's WAY faster than a plain old snow saucer!" I whoop after my first ride.

"I wonder what the speed record is for snow tubes," Francis says.

"Go look it UP, geek," says a gruff voice.

MEANWHILE, **WE'LL** BORROW YOUR NEW **TOY!**

It's Nolan, the kid who ambushed us the other day. And it looks like he's got half the Jefferson wrestling team with him.

"We're using it right now," Teddy tells him.

"Aw, come ON!" Nolan says in a fake, you-just-hurt-my-feelings voice.

He snatches it right out of Teddy's hands. Then he and his crew pile on top of it.

"Hey, get OFF!" Teddy shouts. "It can only hold two people!"

They push off down the hill. But they don't get far. They catch air going over the first bump, and . . .

DISASTER!!

By the time the three of us reach the tube, it's flat as a pancake, and Nolan and his gang are walking away.

"BAD NEWS, chump!" he calls.

It's a helpless feeling. What are we going to do, try and FIGHT them? Those guys are huge. They'd give us the worst face wash we ever had.

Teddy's about to cry, and I don't blame him. "I only got to ride it twice," he says miserably.

"Let's take it back to my house," I say. "We can try to patch it." But we can all see it's beyond patching.

We trudge along in silence until . . .

A bunch of vans and trucks are lined up in front of P.S. 38 like it's afternoon car pool time. What's with all the action on a Saturday?

"That's Dee Dee's dad!" Francis says, pointing to a beefy guy on the sidewalk.

"Eventually," he says. "But first we've got to clean up. It's a MESS in there."

You want to clean up the mold? Easy. Shut down the hot lunch program.

Francis looks puzzled. "But how can we have school with all THAT going on?" he asks.

Dee Dee's dad shrugs. "You CAN'T," he says.

CHAPTER 6

Welcome to the happiest day of my life.

"Yes, I know," Dad says as we all peel off our snow gear. "I just read an email from your principal."

"Does it ALSO explain my master plan for Monday morning?" I ask. "I'm going to wake up early, go stand in the driveway . . ."

Dad shoots me an odd little smile. "Speaking of Jefferson . . ." he begins.

I groan. "Ugh. Can we not talk about Jefferson, Dad? That whole school is Jerk Central."

He raises an eyebrow. "Really?" he asks. Then he shrugs. "All right, I won't say another word."

Huh? Why, so we can read Principal Nichols's thrilling description of mildew in the teachers' lounge? No, thanks. We've got better things to do.

Francis looks at Dad's laptop. "You can forget about that vacation," he says. "Listen to this:"

During the restoration of P.S. 38, no class time will be missed. Our top priority is to make certain that teaching and learning continue without interruption.

"WHAT??" Teddy and I cry in unison.

"In other words, we still have to go to school," Francis says.

"Where, in an IGLOO?" Teddy asks.

Francis keeps reading. "'For the next two weeks, classes will be held on the campus of our sister institution . . .'"

It can't be true. THIS IS AN OUTRAGE!!!

But then Francis and Teddy call home, and guess what? Their parents got the exact same email. What a punch in the gut.

I feel flatter than Teddy's snow tube. Going to another school for two weeks is lousy enough . . . but JEFFERSON?? They already think we're pathetic. This pretty much proves it.

"I'm takin' off," Teddy mutters.

I know what they mean. The day went bad faster than Dad's tuna casserole. I watch them leave, trudge upstairs to my room, and flop onto my bed.

I've been here before. (And no, I don't mean in bed. Duh.) I mean, I've been in a SITUATION like this, where something that SEEMED great turned into a giant turd fest. Here's what happened:

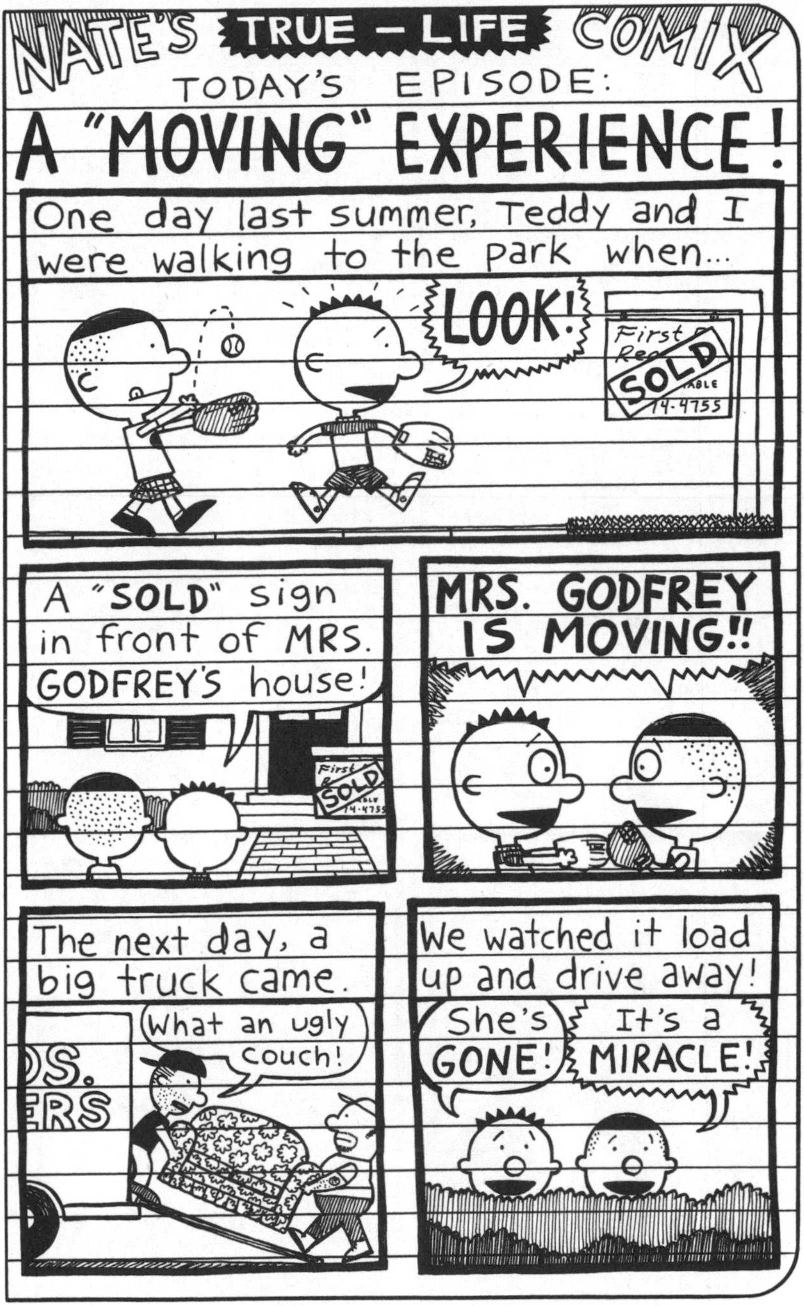
NATE'S TRUE-LIFE COMIX
TODAY'S EPISODE:
A "MOVING" EXPERIENCE!
One day last summer, Teddy and I were walking to the park when...
LOOK!
SOLD
A "SOLD" sign in front of MRS. GODFREY'S house!
MRS. GODFREY IS MOVING!!
The next day, a big truck came.
What an ugly couch!
We watched it load up and drive away!
She's GONE!
It's a MIRACLE!

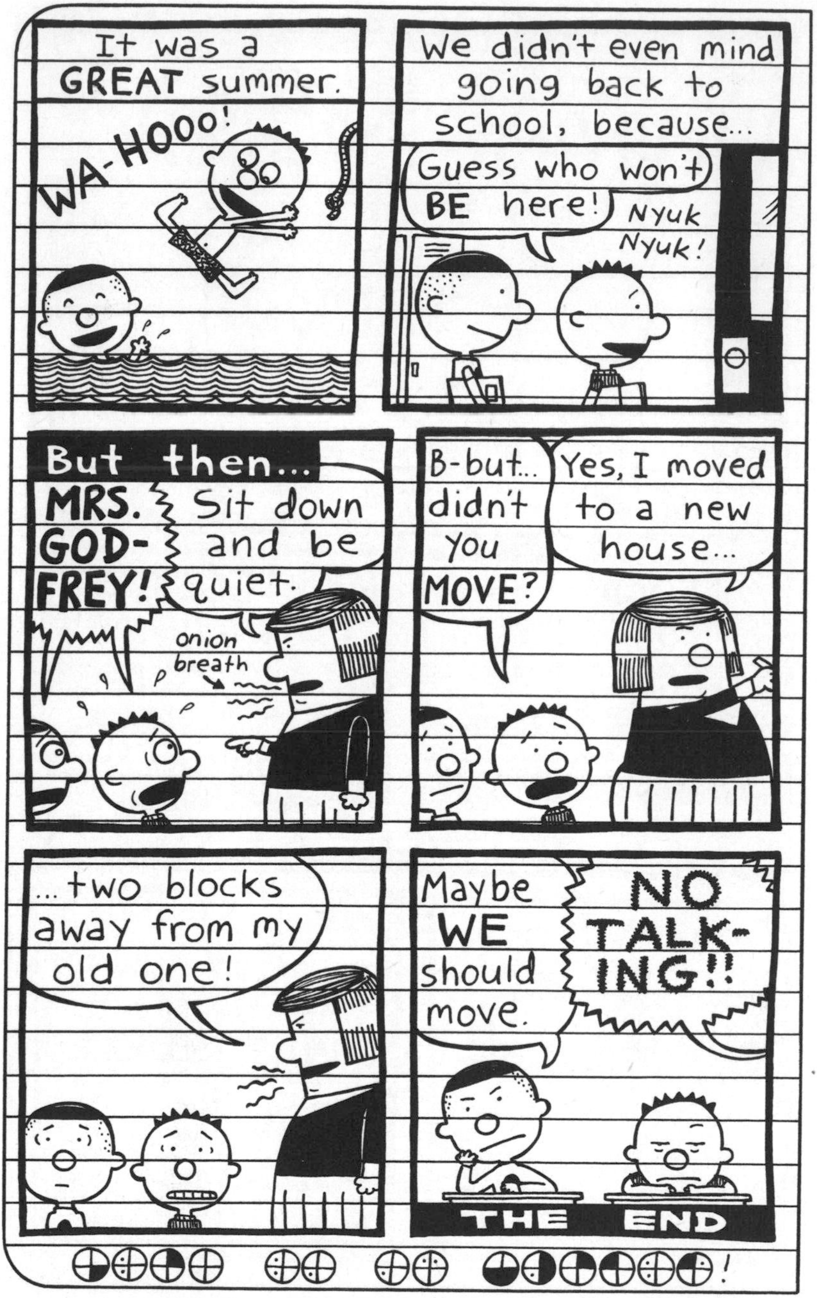
It was a GREAT summer.
WA-HOOO!
We didn't even mind going back to school, because...
Guess who won't BE here!
Nyuk Nyuk!
But then...
MRS. GOD-FREY!
Sit down and be quiet.
onion breath
B-but... didn't you MOVE?
Yes, I moved to a new house...
...two blocks away from my old one!
Maybe WE should move.
NO TALK-ING!!
THE END

My mood hasn't improved much by Monday morning, as the guys and I take the long, slow walk toward Jefferson.

We turn to see Dee Dee running after us. Of course. Who ELSE would scream "yoo-hoo" at 7:30 on a Monday morning?

"EXCITING?" I repeat in disbelief.

"Oh, sure," says Teddy, with a what-planet-are-you-from eye roll.

"I won't mind that one bit!" Dee Dee counters. "When people laugh, it means they NOTICE you!"

That shuts Dee Dee up . . . for maybe two seconds. Then she drops THIS one on us:

We stop dead in our tracks. The three of us stare at her, completely dumbstruck.

"Well, you ARE!" she says. "Why are you so afraid of Jefferson?"

"We're not AFRAID of them," I shoot back.

"Nobody wins ALL the time," she declares.

I'LL BET **OUR** DRAMA CLUB COULD OUTPERFORM **THEIR** DRAMA CLUB!

Ooh. Thanks, Dee Dee. The next time some Jefferson goons are throwing snowballs at my head, I'll remind them that they're no match for P.S. 38 in the vitally important category of musical theater.

Meanwhile, she's still babbling. "All I'm saying is . . ."

EVERYONE CAN BE BEATEN!

EVERYONE HAS AN **ACHILLES' HEEL!**

Okay. Whatever THAT means. I don't really have time to think about it, because . . .

My jaw drops. Holy cow. This is a SCHOOL? It looks more like a MUSEUM.

There are glass cases everywhere, filled from top to bottom with piles of trophies. There are murals painted on the walls and mobiles hanging from the ceiling. There's even a SKYLIGHT. And right in the middle of the lobby, on a huge pedestal . . .

. . . there's a knight.

Sorry. A CAVALIER. They're always bragging that they've got a better mascot than we do . . . and they might be right. Compared to King Arthur here, the stuffed bobcat in the P.S. 38 lobby looks like something we fished out of a Dumpster.

"Welcome to Jefferson Middle School!" booms a voice to our left.

I'M THE PRINCIPAL, MRS. WILLIGER!

...AND I AM **SO HAPPY** YOU'RE HERE!

"So are we!" agrees Dee Dee, who's apparently elected herself our official spokesperson.

"There's still plenty of time before homeroom," Mrs. Williger tells us.

At HOME? Yeah, sure. This place is about as homey as the Grand Canyon.

Francis is right. The more we look around, the more there is to see.

"This is quite a place, isn't it, kids?"

"How come you're HERE?" Teddy asks him. "I thought you were fixing up OUR school."

He chuckles. "I'll leave that to people who know what they're doing . . . like Dee Dee's father."

"So the teachers from P.S. 38 are here at Jefferson, too?" Francis asks.

"Absolutely!" he answers.

Nuts. My chance for a two-week break from Mrs. Godfrey just got flushed.

Sure, bring it on, big fella. Considering how SWANKY this school is . . .

Principal Nichols leads us through a maze of hallways and down a flight of stairs.

"Almost there!" he says cheerfully, as he pushes open a metal door. But hold on . . . what's with the sign that says **EXIT** ?

"This is it!" Principal Nichols announces.

#

We stand at the back door of Jefferson, staring out at . . . um . . . okay, I have no clue. What ARE those things?

"They're modular classrooms, Nate," Principal Nichols explains. "Jefferson used them last fall when they renovated their seventh grade wing . . ."

"Fortunately for us"?? Is he SERIOUS? What's fortunate about going to class in a giant SHOEBOX?

"Think of it as a grand adventure!" he tells us.

Uh . . . no, it won't. Not unless your camp's in the middle of a parking lot. But obviously, Principal Nichols HAS to say that. Making lousy stuff sound good is one of those things ALL grown-ups do.

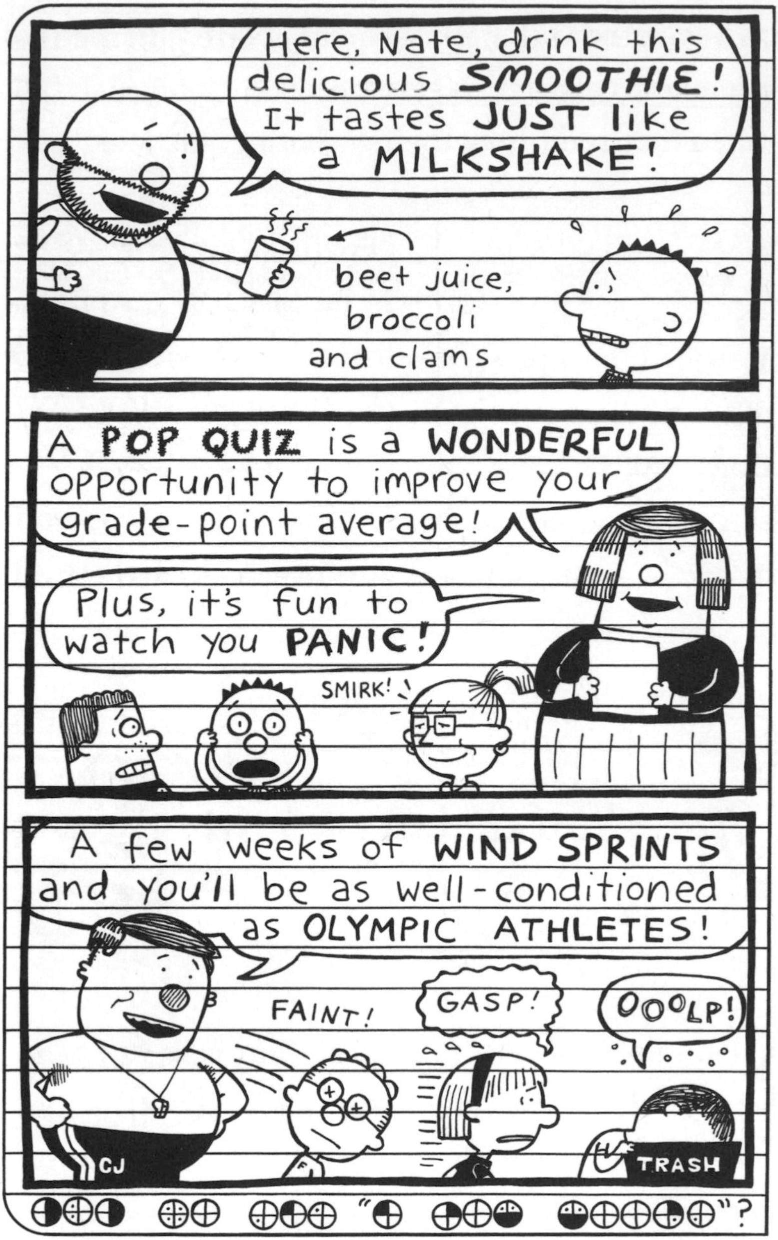
Here, Nate, drink this delicious SMOOTHIE! It tastes JUST like a MILKSHAKE!
beet juice, broccoli and clams
A POP QUIZ is a WONDERFUL opportunity to improve your grade-point average!
Plus, it's fun to watch you PANIC!
SMIRK!
A few weeks of WIND SPRINTS and you'll be as well-conditioned as OLYMPIC ATHLETES!
FAINT!
GASP!
OOOLP!
CJ
TRASH

Principal Nichols steers us toward one of the boxes. "You're in Room F."

"Hear that, Nate?" Teddy cracks. "Room F!"

We swing open the door, and there's Mrs. Godfrey. At P.S. 38, she's always surrounded by books, maps, and other torture devices. Here, all she's got is a flimsy little desk. It feels different.

Different, but exactly the same.

"Hmph," I grumble, looking around. "The REAL classrooms are all tricked out with murals and posters and stuff . . ."

...AND WE DON'T EVEN GET A WINDOW!

Teddy nods. "Yeah, the only thing to look at is . . ." He points silently at Mrs. Godfrey.

"Not exactly a scenic view." I snicker.

"But look at the UPSIDE, guys," Francis chimes in. "Since they've separated us from the Jefferson students . . ."

...WE WON'T HAVE TO LISTEN TO THEM RAG ON US ALL DAY!

Hm. That actually makes sense. As the classroom fills up and the bell rings, it starts to feel like just another brain-frying, butt-numbing school day. By the end of third period, we've almost forgotten we're even AT Jefferson.

And then comes lunch.

Even a fancy-pants school like Jefferson has only one cafetorium. Which means they HAVE to share it with us. When the noon bell rings, we scurry away from our little boxcar

village and into the main building.

"Excuse me, which way to the cafetorium?" Francis asks some Jefferson kid.

"Oh, brother," Teddy mumbles as we continue down the hall. "Can this place get any more stuck-up?"

"Wonder what they call the BATHROOMS," Francis says.

We turn the corner and see a crowd of kids pouring into the cafeteria. (No, I will NOT call it the food court.) That's when it hits us: Something smells . . .

That's weird. We're not used to ANYTHING smelling good in school. Because, frankly, P.S. 38 is the stinkiest place on earth.

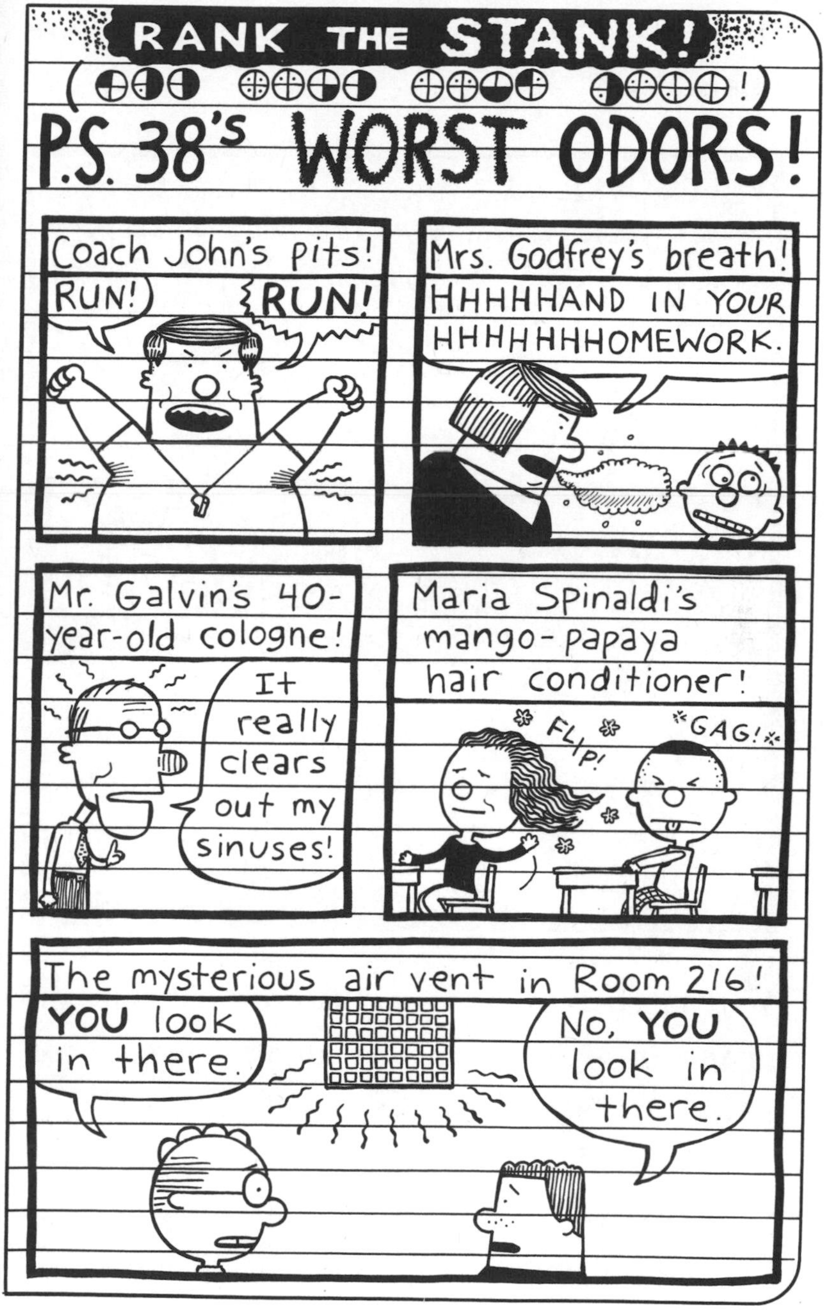
RANK THE STANK!
P.S. 38's WORST ODORS!
Coach John's pits!
RUN!
RUN!
Mrs. Godfrey's breath!
HHHHHAND IN YOUR HHHHHHHOMEWORK.
Mr. Galvin's 40-year-old cologne!
It really clears out my sinuses!
Maria Spinaldi's mango-papaya hair conditioner!
FLIP!
GAG!
The mysterious air vent in Room 216!
YOU look in there.
No, YOU look in there.

"Holy COW!" Teddy exclaims. "Can you believe this MENU?"

We can't believe our eyes. There's not a stewed prune in sight. Okay, we don't have to like Jefferson. But we can like their FOOD.

"What are we waiting for?" Francis says.

I spin around and spot Chad with his tailbone pillow . . . and look who's giving him the evil eye: Nolan. Teddy's right. This IS trouble.

"You're not at P.S. 38 anymore!" he sneers.

That's just wrong. Chad's the smallest kid in the sixth grade. AND he's hurt. The last thing he needs is a scuzzbucket like Nolan piling on.

"Or maybe it's NOT a toilet seat!" Nolan laughs.

I look for a teacher, but there aren't any. Typical. When you don't want them around, they're on you like white on rice. But when you actually NEED one? Good luck.

I feel my hands curl into fists. I'm no match for Nolan. But SOMEBODY'S got to help Chad.

She marches over to Nolan and sticks her finger right in his chest. "You give him back his pillow!" she demands.

Nolan does a quick three sixty to make sure no teachers are watching. Then he slaps Dee Dee's hand away. "Beat it," he growls.

"Dee Dee's going to get herself killed," Francis says. I take a deep breath.

We park ourselves next to Dee Dee and Chad. "Come on, Nolan," Teddy says. "Knock it off."

He laughs right in Teddy's face. "Why?" he asks.

Hm. Okay, so much for Dad's bully theory.

Thanks for the wisdom, Dad. I'll file that away with all your other brilliant theories, like "Making your bed every day helps you live longer" and

"If you really get to know her, Mrs. Godfrey is probably a very nice person."

"Give it here!" Dee Dee says suddenly, trying to snatch the pillow from Nolan. But he's too quick for her.

He tosses it toward one of his crew, but it veers the tiniest bit off target.

By the time I realize I'm losing my balance, it's too late. There's no way to stop myself. Look out below.

Oof. I lie there stunned, hoping I didn't just join Chad in the bruised tailbone club.

"Good gravy! Nate, are you all right?" It's Principal Nichols. Great timing. NOW he shows up?

Mrs. Williger is here, too. But she doesn't look quite as friendly as she did this morning.

"Horseplay?" I protest. "But I wasn't . . ."

"We'll sort it out later, Nate," Principal Nichols tells me. "Let's get you up on your feet."

"What hurts?" he asks.

"My wrist!" I groan. I try to flex it, and the pain hits about a fifty on a scale of one to ten.

"Is he going to live?" asks Dee Dee.

"I think he'll make it," says Principal Nichols, lifting me off the floor.

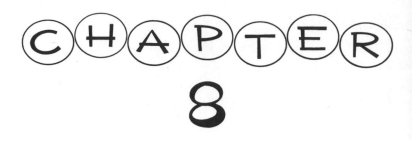

CHAPTER 8

"You know, that's not a bad joke," Teddy says as we file into the art room the next morning. "For a principal."

"Joke, shmoke," I grumble. "What's funny about a broken wrist?"

Oh, sure, Francis, it's a RIOT. And having a hunk of plaster wrapped around my hand for the next month should be a barrel of laughs.

I used to think it might be kind of COOL to have a cast. Last year, when Eric Fleury broke his arm, everyone treated him like Joe

Celebrity. All the girls were lining up for Eric time.

Suddenly the guy was a total babe magnet. (And, PS: All he did was fall down in the school yard while doing cheesy kung fu moves! At least I got hurt trying to help Chad.)

Anyway, Eric's moment of glory lasted about three minutes. After that, he said having a cast

turned into a major pain—and, boy, was he right. This thing is hot. It itches like crazy. And it's already starting to smell like Coach John's tube socks.

But you know the worst part about it? It's on my right hand. My DRAWING hand.

Brilliant deduction, Chad. There's only one little problem: I CAN'T DRAW!!

Oh, I've TRIED. It's the first thing I did when I got home from the hospital yesterday. But I can't even hold a pencil with this stupid cast on. It's like wearing a cement mitten.

So then I went with plan B: drawing left-handed.

Pathetic, right? I did better drawings back in KINDERGARTEN. And Dad made it worse by doing that fake praise thing parents always do. I hate that.

So now you know why I'm not exactly turning cartwheels when Mr. Rosa tells us to get to work. But I give it a shot.

"Maybe you should try sticking the pencil up your nose," Teddy cracks, after watching me draw a dog that looks more like a radioactive spider. ➡

"Maybe YOU should," I snap back.

"I don't have a broken wrist," he reminds me.

THAT COULD CHANGE.

"Okay, everyone, five-minute warning!" Mr. Rosa calls out. As we all start cleaning up, he stops by our table.

"Do you kids remember Mrs. Everett?" he asks.

"Sure!" says Francis. "She came to our Doodlers meeting!"

WELL, HER CLUB, THE C.I.C., IS MEETING TODAY...

...AND WE'RE INVITED!

OOOOOH! LUCKY US!

When science ends (and not a moment too soon, because Mr. Galvin was about to hit a new low on the Charisma meter), the Doodlers head for Mrs. Everett's room . . .

. . . along with our newest member.

THIS IS SO **EXCITING!** I'VE NEVER BEEN TO A CARTOONING CLUB MEETING! WHAT DO YOU THINK IT'LL BE LIKE? HOW MANY KIDS FROM JEFFERSON WILL BE THERE? I CAN'T WAIT TO SEE EVERYONE'S COMICS! HAVE YOU EVER MET ANY FAMOUS CARTOONISTS? WHAT IF **I** BECOME A FAMOUS CARTOONIST SOMEDAY?

Dee Dee's yapping like a Chihuahua on a sugar buzz. I guess she's all amped up about listening to the almighty C.I.C. tell us how TALENTED they are. Or maybe she can't wait to see one of my amazingly lame left-handed drawings.

"It seems pretty quiet," Teddy says as we approach an open doorway. "Are you sure we're in the right place?"

"You're ABSOLUTELY in the right place!" says Mrs. Everett, waving us into the room.

Here's a shocker: Jefferson has the swankiest art studio I've ever seen. And it's packed with kids drawing comics.

A few look up and nod, but most of them don't even notice us. They just keep drawing. Wow, it's like an ASSEMBLY LINE in here.

"Yes." Mrs. Everett nods. "They have a deadline."

"It's a local literary magazine," Mrs. Everett explains. "It's sponsoring a kids' writing contest!"

Chad looks baffled. "But . . . comics aren't WRITING!"

"SURE they are!" she says.

"I have entry forms, if you're interested," she adds.

"I'll be right back." Mrs. Everett smiles.

Everybody chatters excitedly as she goes to her desk. Except me. I don't say a word.

"What's wrong with this picture?" Teddy asks.

"Huh?" I mumble.

"Because I can't enter the CONTEST, Einstein,"
I answer. "I'm halfway through my most hilarious
'Doctor Cesspool' adventure EVER . . . "

Mrs. Everett is back. "Why not collaborate?" she
suggests. "You could write the rest of the story,
and couldn't one of your fellow Doodlers supply
the artwork?"

What? Whoa, WHOA. No offense, Dee Dee, but you're not exactly at the top of my A-list. I'll team up with Francis or Teddy or . . .

"I think that's a GREAT idea!" Mr. Rosa just appeared out of nowhere at our table.

Oh, come on. I already took her to the dance and carried her home on my back. Haven't I suffered enough? But Mr. Rosa's wearing his happy adviser face. Nuts. I guess it's settled.

"Just hand them back by Friday, along with your comics!"

Dee Dee scoots her chair over next to mine. "Tell me about Doctor Cesspool! What's his story?"

"Yeah, but this isn't the Drama Club!" I hiss at her. "It's . . . it's . . ." My voice trails off.

"What's the matter?" she whispers.

I look around the room at all the Jefferson kids bent over their drawings.

I'm not used to this. Doodlers meetings are FUN. Mr. Rosa lets us talk and play the radio and eat snacks. This is different.

"You're right, Nate, it IS awfully quiet," Mr. Rosa says. Then he gives me a wink. "But maybe the Doodlers can find a way to liven things up!"

He walks over to Mrs. Everett. "May we show you and your students a fun drawing game?"

"Of course!" she answers.

"Grab a fresh sheet of paper, everyone!" Mr. Rosa announces.

"You'll figure it out as we go along!" Mr. Rosa tells them. "At the end of the game, you'll have drawn a complete character from head to toe!"

"Except the characters might not HAVE heads!" Chad laughs. "OR toes!"

"I'll go first!" I say. "Draw . . . ummmm . . ."

". . . and that's ALL you draw!" Mr. Rosa says. "Until the NEXT person tells us what to add on! How 'bout it, Teddy?"

"Ah!" Mr. Rosa exclaims. "So now it's up to YOU, cartoonists, to decide exactly WHERE to draw that peg leg!"

One Jefferson kid looks confused. "My drawing is just a nose and a peg leg, floating in space."

"Perfect! You're doing it right!" says Mr. Rosa. "Who's next?"

Like I always say: There's nothing like a game of Add-On to break the ice. When the time comes for everyone to show off their drawings, we're all cracking up. Every single drawing is completely hilarious. And believe it or not, guess whose is my favorite?

"That was FABULOUS!" Dee Dee says as we leave Mrs. Everett's room an hour later. "I should have joined the Doodlers YEARS ago!"

"We didn't EXIST years ago," Francis points out.

"It was a good meeting," I say, "once those C.I.C. kids actually started TALKING to us."

"Yeah, some of them were pretty nice!" Dee Dee agrees. "SEE, you guys . . . ?"

CHAPTER 9

Wowza! A girl is walking . . .

No, wait. Let me start again.

A TURBO CUTE girl is walking this way, and . . .

. . . she's looking right at ME! JACKPOT!!

"You're Nate, right?" she asks.

"Very smooth," Teddy mutters. I give him a quick kick in the shin.

"I just want to tell you," the mystery girl says, "everyone thought it was GREAT the way you stood up to Nolan in the food court yesterday!"

So THIS is what it was like for Eric Fleury. "Sure!" I say. "I think I've got a pen here somewhere . . ."

"Oh, I've got one," she says quickly, pulling out a marker the size of a salami.

Wait, what? She disappears around the corner, and I hear an explosion of laughter. A vise tightens in my stomach as I look down at my wrist.

Then she's back. Only this time, she's not alone.

Away they go, laughing their heads off. Bet you a buck they're not discussing knock-knock jokes.

"That was tricky dirt," Artur says.

"You mean 'dirty trick,'" says Francis.

Dee Dee throws up her hands. "Don't blame ME!" she protests. "I was just trying to look on the BRIGHT side!"

"There IS no bright side." Chad sighs.

What ABOUT it? I'll be watching from the bench. I can't play basketball with this giant plaster sweatband on my wrist.

"Wait, won't the game be postponed?" Francis asks. "The gym at P.S. 38 is in no condition to—"

Teddy cuts him off. "We're not playing at P.S. 38. They're moving the game HERE. To Jefferson."

NOW what? Is this another example of Dee Dee's terminal case of Look-at-Me-itis, or . . .

"No," she says, hands on her hips. "I'm simply pointing out how useless it is to stand around complaining . . ."

Apparently, while I wasn't paying attention, Dee Dee became a basketball expert. "Okay, then, Coach," I say sarcastically. "How DO we win?"

"By finding Jefferson's weakness, of course."

FINDING THEIR **WEAKNESS**!!! **JEEPERS**, WHY DIDN'T **I** THINK OF THAT? IT'S SO **SIMPLE**!!

"I never said it was simple," she tells me. "But Jefferson's not indestructible."

? ?

THEY'VE **GOT** TO HAVE AN **ACHILLES' HEEL**!

That's the SECOND time she's said that. Who's this Achilles dude? And what does his HEEL have to do with anything?

Later, at home, I decide to find out.

"Dad," I ask, "what's an Achilles' heel?"

Who asked YOU, Ellen? But before I can stop her, she's shoving some papers in my face. "I wrote this report in fourth grade!" she brags.

Difference number 7,387,289 between me and Ellen: The reports I did in fourth grade are buried in a landfill somewhere. The ones SHE did are carefully stored in a file cabinet in her room, right next to her priceless collection of plastic panda figurines.

The Myth Of
ACHILLES A+ ☺

by Ellen Wright   Grade 4

In ancient Greece, the goddess **Thetis** fell in love with a mortal named **Peleus**. They had a son and named him **Achilles**.

When Achilles was a baby, Thetis decided that she wanted Achilles to be immortal like she was, so she carried him to the **River Styx**. Everything that touched the river's magical waters became **indestructible.**

Thetis held Achilles by the heel and dipped him in the river, not realizing that his **HEEL** never touched the water!!!

Achilles grew up and became the greatest warrior in the land. The **Trojan War** was being fought between Greece and Troy. Achilles was on the side of the

(turn page!!) ⟶

Greeks. At first, Achilles re-
fused to fight because he was
mad at **Agamemnon**, the leader
of the Greek army. But after
his best friend **Patroclus** was
killed, Achilles joined the battle.
    Thousands and thousands of
Trojan arrows struck Achilles, but
they had no effect. <u>THEN</u>...

    One arrow hit him in the **HEEL** -
the only part of his body left
untouched by the protective waters
of the River Styx!! Because of
that, Achilles died.
    So when people say something is
your **"Achilles' heel,"** they mean it's
a tiny weakness that might cause
you <u>big</u> trouble. I think that's
interesting!! Don't **YOU**????
              The End

Huh. Yeah, that IS pretty interesting. But why should I tell HER that? It's not my job to inflate Ellen's ego. She's got her own built-in pump.

There's the doorbell. I'll get it.

Until this very second, I thought Dee Dee was a little unusual. Okay, maybe more than a little . . . but basically harmless. Now I'm not so sure.

She might have some deeper issues.

"Why are you dressed like a cat?" I ask her. I COULD have said: "Have you completely lost your mind?"

"I'm doing a dress rehearsal!" she answers happily. "And I'm not just ANY cat! . . ."

"I'm going to wear this to the game Saturday and cheer us on to victory! I'll be our mascot!"

"Are you CRAZY?" I shout. "You can't show up at Jefferson looking like THAT!"

"Well, of COURSE not, silly!" she says.

ON **GAME NIGHT**, I'LL BE WEARING **MAKEUP!** AND <u>WHISKERS!</u>

"But bobcats are FIERCE!" I tell her. "You look like you should be rolling around on the floor with a ball of YARN!"

"Oh, pshaw," she says.

"PSHAW"?

LET'S TALK ABOUT OUR **CARTOONING COLLABORATION!**

"If I'm going to finish your 'Doctor Cesspool' story in time to enter the contest, I'd better get started!"

Oh, right, I forgot about that.

DEE DEE'S IMITATION OF A GIANT **FUR BALL** GAVE ME A **BRAIN CRAMP!**

I grab a bunch of paper from my room. But I don't like this. What if Dee Dee totally messes up my comic? What if she makes it all . . . well . . . DEE DEE-ish?

THE FIRST PART'S ALL DONE... AND THE SECOND PART I SKETCHED LIGHTLY IN PENCIL. SO ALL YOU HAVE TO DO IS FINISH IT IN PEN. YOU DON'T HAVE TO... UH... ADD ANY WEIRD DETAILS, OR... I MEAN... JUST DON'T DO ANY... ANYTHING... UM... Y'KNOW... ANY CHANGES OR... UH... WHAT I MEAN IS...

"Nate, RELAX!" she says. "I'm not going to ruin your comic!"

So what happens? Two days later, Dee Dee submits "Doctor Cesspool" WITHOUT EVEN SHOWING ME THE FINISHED COMIC!

"I didn't have TIME to show it to you!" she explains at the end of school on Friday.

It's not that I don't believe her. It's just that I wanted to SEE it first. After all, "Doctor Cesspool" is MY creation.

But what's done is done. I can't do anyth—

"In here!" whispers a voice.

"Chad?" Dee Dee says. "Is that you?"

"Yeah!" he whispers back. "Come on in! . . ."

Dee Dee and I squeeze inside.

"Close the door, you guys," says Chad. "I don't think we're supposed to be in here."

It's basically a king-size closet, packed with all sorts of stuff: old science equipment that looks like its last stop was Frankenstein's lab, a couple of antique bicycles, a lawn mower, a stuffed owl . . .

"Ooh!" Dee Dee says . . .

A **SUIT** OF **ARMOR!**

"ANOTHER one?"
I say. "They've
already got one
on display in
the front hall!"

"Yeah," Chad says. "Why do they need TWO?"

"Because they're twice as good as everyone else," I grumble. "They're JEFFERSON."

"Hiding," he answers.

"Hiding?" I ask as I pop back into the hallway.

"THERE you are, Tiny!" Nolan sneers at Chad.

"We weren't playing any games," I say through gritted teeth.

"Oh, that's right, I FORGOT!" Nolan crows. "P.S. 38 STINKS at games!"

"The only thing you'll find out is that a BOBCAT is no match for a CAVALIER!" Nolan says.

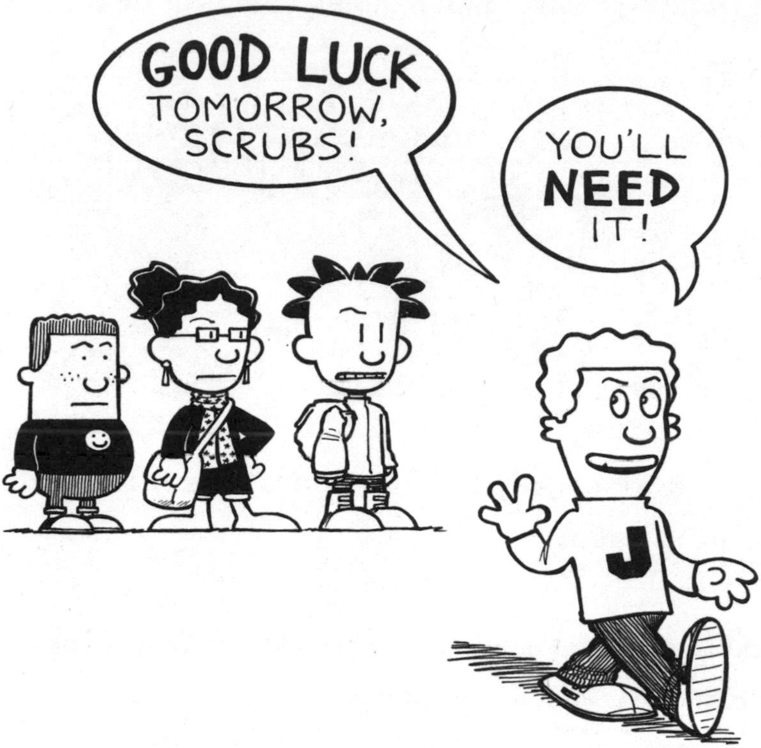
GOOD LUCK TOMORROW, SCRUBS!
YOU'LL NEED IT!

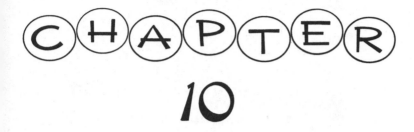

CHAPTER 10

You can't always believe everything you see. Like this scoreboard, for instance.

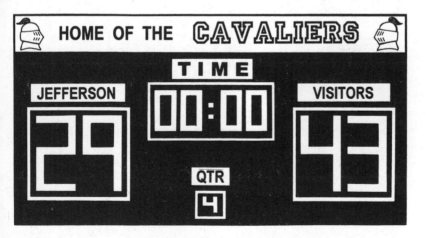

You're probably thinking: Wow! P.S. 38 did it! They beat Jefferson, 43–29!

Uh, wrong.

See, the scoreboard only has room for TWO-DIGIT numbers. We scored 43, all right. But Jefferson didn't score 29. They scored . . .

And all I could do was sit there and WATCH it. I felt like running onto the court and clubbing somebody over the head with my cast . . . but I stopped myself. I didn't want to rebreak my wrist.

Chad was on the bench beside me, taking pictures for the yearbook. Great. We can stick these on a page called "most humiliating moments."

Poor Coach. He's usually Peter Positive, but he looked like he'd just lost (a) his dog, (b) his best friend, and (c) a basketball game . . . BY EIGHTY-SIX POINTS!!

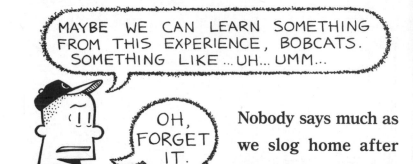

Nobody says much as we slog home after the game. Except Francis. Every time we lose to Jefferson, he has to analyze exactly what went wrong.

"Offense, defense, rebounding . . ." he says. "They beat us in every part of the game."

"But they didn't HAVE a mascot," Chad says.

"Exactly!" answers Dee Dee. "So I won!"

"That's ridiculous," Francis says.

"Guys!" I shout. "Let's DO it!"

"Do what?" everyone asks.

"Right!" I say. "They've spanked us at all the OFFICIAL activities . . ."

Francis is skeptical. "Like what?" he asks.

"Leave that to ME!" I tell him.

Have you ever read the Great Brain books? They're awesome. The main character, Tom, is a genius. Like me. And whenever he has a problem that needs solving, he thinks about it right before he goes to bed. Then his Great Brain comes up with a perfect solution while he sleeps. When he wakes up in the morning, he's got an answer.

Except it doesn't work. When I open my eyes at 8:00 a.m. . . . .

. . . all I can remember is that I was having a dream about Mrs. Godfrey drowning in an ocean of Cheez Doodles. But no great ideas. No perfect solutions. I guess my brain took the night off.

And the morning, too. The hours roll by, and I'm still stumped. I haven't felt this clueless since that last science test. (Who CARES about the digestive system of a fruit fly?) Anyway, I need help.

And I know just who to ask. Someone with experience. Someone who knows what he's talking about.

Mr. Rosa will understand. After all, he's been teaching at P.S. 38 since before I was BORN.

I cut right to the chase. "We want to challenge Jefferson to . . . um . . . something."

"Hm," he says. "What kind of something?"

"That's what I can't figure out," I admit.

"Well, nobody's good at EVERYTHING," he says. "And don't sell P.S. 38 short. Remember, YOU have strengths, TOO."

"Think of that C.I.C. meeting we went to the other day," he explains. "Didn't you think it was kind of BORING?"

"Oh yeah, it was a no-fun zone in there," I agree, "until we showed them how to play Add-On."

"Right. By the way, who taught YOU that game?"

Mr. Rosa smiles. "I see," he says. "Very creative."

Then he pulls two booklets out of a drawer and lays them on the table. "You might recognize one of these," he tells me.

"It sure is," he says. "And the other is a collection of drawings by the Jefferson C.I.C. Take a look."

I get that familiar queasy feeling in my stomach as I flip through the booklet.

"They can really draw," is all I can say.

"Oh, yes, they're very good," Mr. Rosa agrees.

"Huh? There are no STORIES in here," I say, scanning the booklet again. "Just drawings."

"Right," he says. "But YOUR booklet is FULL of stories. Some very FUNNY stories, by the way!"

"I repeat," Mr. Rosa says, his eyes twinkling. "Very creative."

"Yeah, but . . . I still don't know what kind of competition to have with Jefferson!" I say as Mr. Rosa shows me to the door.

"You'll think of something," he says simply.

Strengths. Okay, I get the message: I'm creative. But how's that going to help us beat Jefferson in any kind of showdown?

THAT'S IT! Maybe I didn't find an answer in my sleep like the Great Brain, but I figured something out eventually. It just goes to show . . .

I slam into Dee Dee, who for some reason is standing right in the middle of the sidewalk. "Oh, my LEG!" she moans as she gets to her feet. "I think I FRACTURED my KNEECAP!"

"Save the drama for your mama, Dee Dee," I say, "and listen to this great idea!"

Her face lights up as I describe my plan, and pretty soon she's hopping around like Spitsy with a kibble buzz. So much for that fractured kneecap.

When we get to Dee Dee's, she pulls out some poster board and markers and gets to work. I call the guys to fill them in. We all agree: This is our best chance ever to finally beat Jefferson.

First thing Monday morning, we do a little decorating in the Jefferson lobby.

"You're challenging us to a snow sculpture contest?" Nolan sneers.

"Surprise," Teddy whispers in my ear.

"We're not planning on losing," Dee Dee answers.

One of Nolan's groupies shoots us a suspicious look. "How do we decide who wins?"

"One judge from each school. That's fair," Francis says.

Nolan shrugs. "Whatever. It's not going to matter WHO the judges are . . ."

They walk off, leaving us standing in the ginormous lobby full of trophies, plaques, and championship banners.

Chad looks worried. "They seem pretty confident."

"Yeah," I say. "But not as confident as I am."

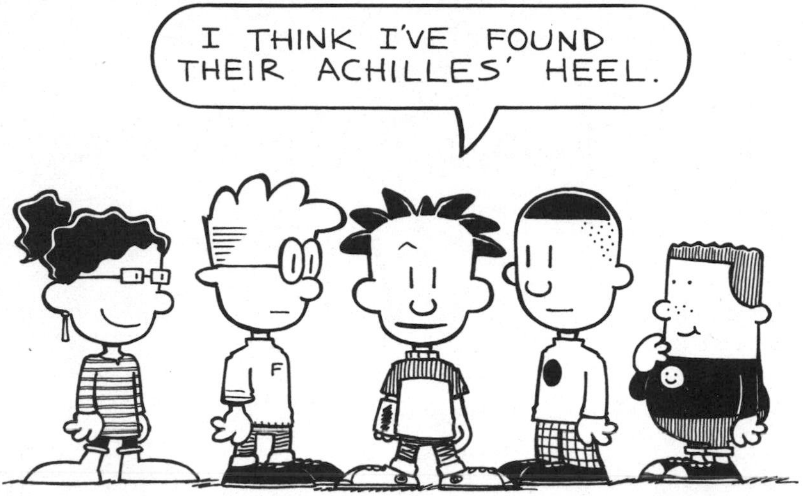
I THINK I'VE FOUND THEIR ACHILLES' HEEL.

CHAPTER

11

The school is buzzing all week until—FINALLY!—
Saturday's here. The air's cold but not TOO cold.
The snow's wet but not TOO wet. It's perfect sculp-
ture weather.

All of us swing into action. By "us," I mean us KIDS. The Ultimate Snowdown is for kids only. We don't want a bunch of grown-ups trying to hog the glory. You know what happens when so-called adults try to take over. ➤

Besides, it's not like we need any more people. We've got tons of kids ready to roll, and so does Jefferson. At least I THINK they do. It's hard to tell, because . . .

"What's THAT all about?" Teddy asks.

"Maybe they think we'll try to copy their sculpture," Francis says.

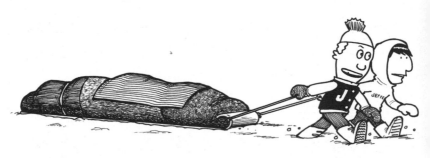

Nolan and another kid sneak out from behind the school, pulling a sled loaded up with . . . well, whatever it is, it's all covered in blankets. We watch as they disappear behind the tarp.

"I wonder what that was," Chad says.

"Maybe it was a dead body," Dee Dee whispers.

"If we stand around yakking about what JEFFERSON's doing, we'll never finish OUR sculpture!" Francis says.

Reality check: We've only got six hours. If we want to create a masterpiece by 3:00 this afternoon . . .

So we do. Once we stop worrying about that giant tarp, we start humming along like a well-oiled machine. Some kids toss snow on the pile, others pack it down, and those of us with actual

artistic talent do the rest. Our sculpture starts to take shape. And (I'm not just saying this because it was my idea) it looks AWESOME.

I think it'll be good enough . . . if my theory about Jefferson's weak spot is right. But we're not going to find out for sure until . . .

"Let's start with Jefferson's entry," Mr. Rosa says.

A couple of kids from the C.I.C. start to lower the tarp. I hold my breath. This is it: almighty Jefferson's moment of truth.

The cheers from Jefferson almost blow my ears off. Our side looks stunned. There's no doubt: It's a pretty amazing sculpture.

But I'm not looking at the cavalier. I'm looking at
Mr. Rosa and Mrs. Everett. And you know what?

The two of them inspect
the sculpture from every
angle. Then they put their
heads together, talking in
whispers. Finally . . .

"There's a real suit of armor under here," Mr. Rosa says.

It gets deadly quiet. I sneak a peek at Nolan. He looks . . . NERVOUS.

"That explains the impressive degree of realism," Mrs. Everett says. She turns to Nolan. "Did you use the old suit of armor from the storage room?"

She nods. "That's true. Technically, no rules were broken. But just covering something with snow instead of sculpting it yourselves . . ."

"I KNEW it!" I whisper.

Chad looks puzzled. "You knew they were going to swipe that suit of armor?"

I shake my head. "No, but I knew they're not as CREATIVE as we are!"

We wade through the snow toward our sculpture. Mr. Rosa taps me on the shoulder. "Nate, tell us about P.S. 38's entry."

"Sure!" I answer. "It's called . . ."

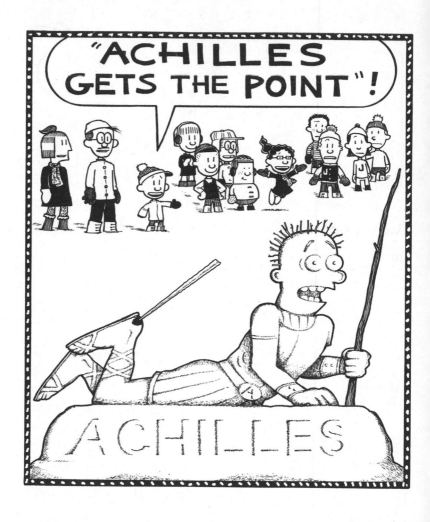

"What a dynamic pose!" Mrs. Everett exclaims. "And I love the expression on his face!"

"How did you make the arrow?" Mr. Rosa asks, glancing at the Jefferson kids. "Did you pack snow around a REAL arrow?"

Mrs. Everett studies the blotch of red on Achilles' heel. "This isn't actual blood, I hope?"

"Well, you SUCCEEDED!" Mrs. Everett laughs. Then she nods at Mr. Rosa. He nods back. Here it comes.

"The judges are in agreement!" she announces.

"The winners of the Ultimate Snowdown ARE . . ."

We explode. Everyone goes crazy. I mean, CRAZY. Teddy's throwing handfuls of snow, Chad's doing snow angels, and Dee Dee's hugging anything that moves. Me? I just keep pinching myself. We finally did it. WE BEAT JEFFERSON!!!

Mrs. Everett finds me in the crowd. "Nate, congratulations! You and your classmates did a wonderful job!"

"Thanks," I say, ducking out of the way of a bear hug from Dee Dee.

"I'm curious, though," she says. "Why did you choose Achilles as a subject?"

"We just think it's a good story," I tell her. "Achilles thought he was indestructible. But the truth is . . ."

CHAPTER 12

P.S. 38 finally reopened on Monday. I never thought I'd say this, but . . .

"Nate and Dee Dee, you won third prize in the 'Story Spinners' kids' writing competition!"

"That means we beat Jefferson AGAIN!" I crow.

"Yes," Mr. Rosa says with a smile. "You've got a winning streak going!"

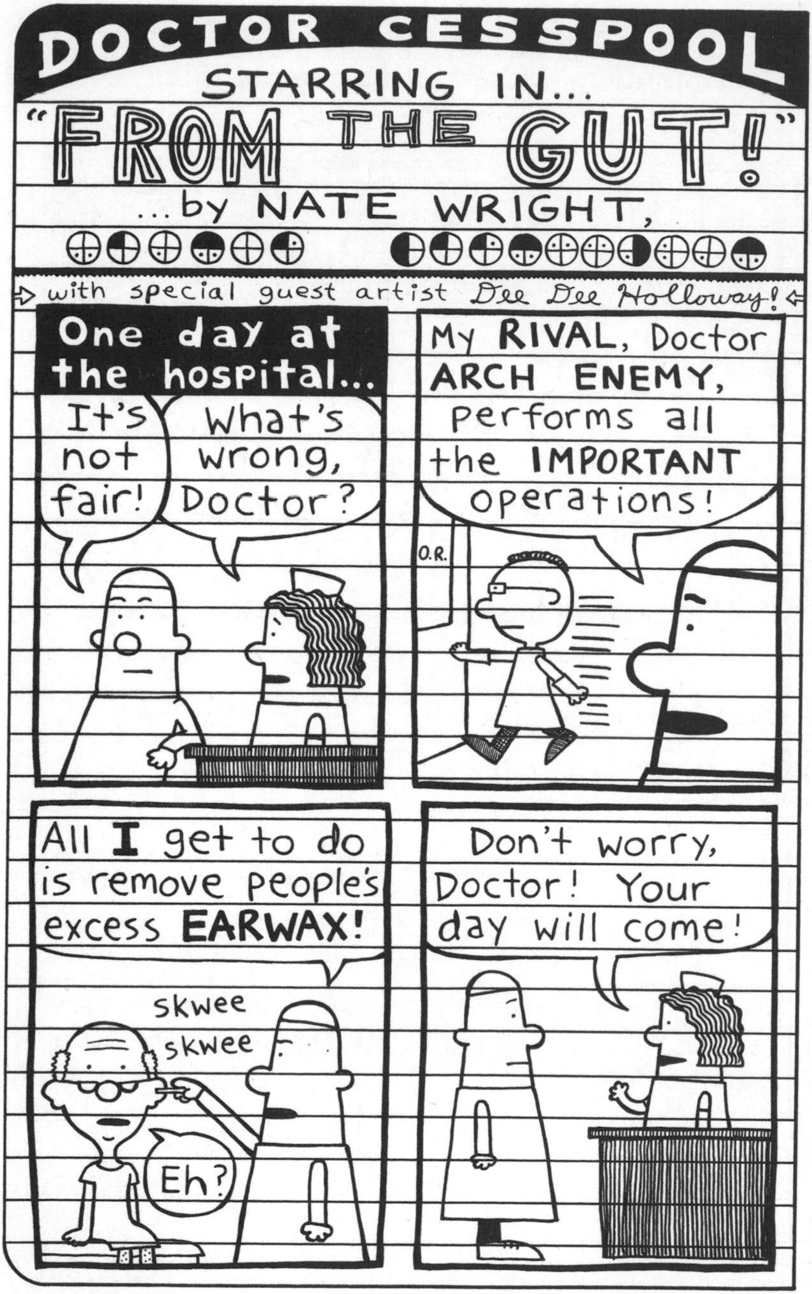
DOCTOR CESSPOOL
STARRING IN...
"FROM THE GUT!"
...by NATE WRIGHT,
with special guest artist Dee Dee Holloway!
One day at the hospital...
It's not fair!
What's wrong, Doctor?
My RIVAL, Doctor ARCH ENEMY, performs all the IMPORTANT operations!
O.R.
All I get to do is remove people's excess EARWAX!
skwee skwee
Eh?
Don't worry, Doctor! Your day will come!

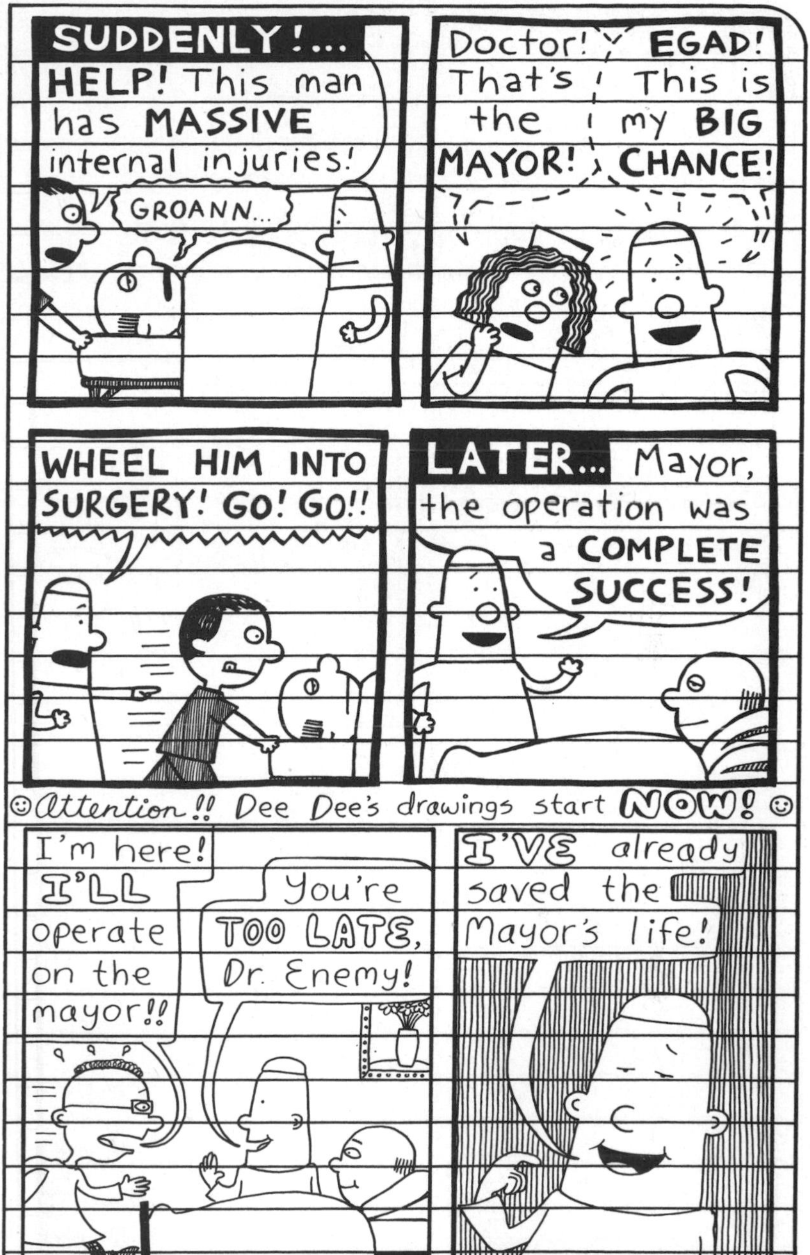

SUDDENLY!...
HELP! This man has MASSIVE internal injuries!
GROANN...
Doctor! That's the MAYOR!
EGAD! This is my BIG CHANCE!
WHEEL HIM INTO SURGERY! GO! GO!!
LATER...
Mayor, the operation was a COMPLETE SUCCESS!
☺Attention!! Dee Dee's drawings start NOW!☺
I'm here! I'LL operate on the mayor!!
You're TOO LATE, Dr. Enemy!
I'VE already saved the Mayor's life!

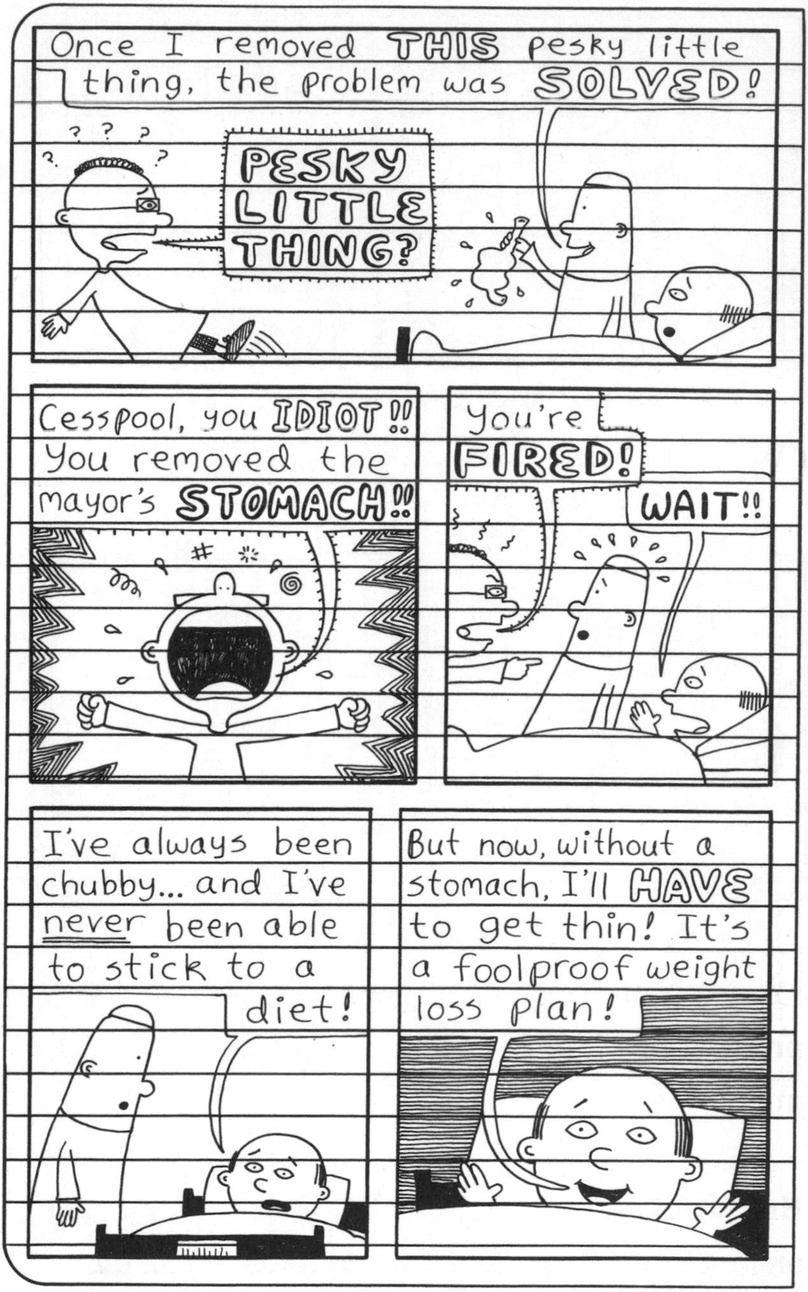
Once I removed THIS pesky little thing, the problem was SOLVED!
PESKY LITTLE THING?
Cesspool, you IDIOT!! You removed the mayor's STOMACH!!
You're FIRED!
WAIT!!
I've always been chubby... and I've never been able to stick to a diet!
But now, without a stomach, I'll HAVE to get thin! It's a foolproof weight loss plan!

"Wow!" I exclaim. "It turned out . . . GREAT!"

"Yeah, it's UNIQUE! I bet that's why you got a prize!" Francis says. "If you hadn't teamed up, you might not have won ANYTHING!"

Hm. Maybe that's true. Maybe without this cast on my wrist, none of this would have happened.

And it all started with my swan dive off that table in the Jefferson food court. Pretty funny, right? It was a total accident.

READ ALL THE BIG NATE BOOKS TODAY!

NOVELS

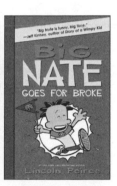

READ ALL THE BiGNATE BOOKS TODAY!

ACTIVITY BOOKS

COMIC COMPILATIONS

HARPER
An Imprint of HarperCollinsPublishers

WWW.BIGNATEBOOKS.CO